DREAMING THE MARSH

by

Elizabeth McCulloch

ISBN # 978-1-940189-26-0

Library of Congress Control Number: 2019937869

This is a work of fiction. Any resemblance to real events or persons, living or dead, is entirely coincidental.

Author photos by Adrienne Fletcher Photography

Twisted Road Publications

Twisted Road
PUBLICATIONS

DREAMING THE MARSH

To Mary Anne Hilker, friend and first reader

The Marsh

South of Opakulla, along the straight gray strip of 226, between the "Guns" sign and Missitucknee, stretches the Marsh, old as time. Once it was an ocean, home to fish and the sliding shadows of sharks. Then the ocean fell away, and the sharks left their fierce teeth behind. Rain turned the salt lakes to fresh, ran creeks across the land, seeped down through the lime rock, cut and filled great caverns underground. Grasses, brush, trees and vines grew up and steamed in the Florida sun. Camels grazed in the grasslands; mastodons splashed in the shallow lakes. Millenia melted away, and children playing in the snaky scrub, slapping mosquitoes on their damp faces, found the ancient bones and told stories of giants in the Marsh.

The Marsh is full of stories; the Marsh is full of magic....

A boy sat by the fire as the men burned out the great pine log to make a canoe. Grown, he felled and hollowed a smooth cypress trunk and carved pictures in the charred wood: an alligator slipping around the bow, a great blue heron flying above the stern. As he glided through the shallow marsh lakes in the dawn mists, the fish swam to his canoe. From that day, all his people made their canoes from cypress, and carved them with beasts and birds. The Great Cypress Island became a sacred place, and each boy in his turn spent three days and nights in among the trees, waiting for one to call him.

A cattle rancher lay dying in the bed where he was born. From his window he looked out over the great grasslands of the Marsh, to the blue line of Cypress Lake on the horizon. He had burned the woods to clear land for grazing, dammed a stream to give his boys a swimming hole. But he would not harvest the ancient cypress. His sons pressed

1

him to sell, gave him no peace. He swore that if they cut the trees, they would lose the land.

Fifty years went by, and his foolish grandchildren began the harvest. And so, by the terms of his will, the land became the Missitucknee Marsh State Park. It was twenty thousand acres, give or take a few, of grassland and oak hammock, water-filled sinkholes, and broad shallow lakes connected by streams.

And these are the fish that lived in the Marsh: speckled perch, blue gill, bream, sunfish, largemouth bass, short-nosed gar.

And these are the reptiles that lived in the Marsh: alligators, softshell turtles, stinkpot turtles, cooters, watersnakes, black racers, diamondback rattlers, water moccasins.

And these are the birds that lived in the Marsh: great blue herons, white ibis, least bitterns, limpkins, anhingas, ducks, moor hens, purple gallinules, cormorants, wood storks, ospreys, red shouldered hawks, barred owls.

And these are the mammals that lived in the Marsh: raccoons, deer, possum, rabbits, otters, squirrels, bobcats, skunks, bats, and people.

One

The sun popped up there at the edge of the world, stretching long warm fingers across the Marsh, erasing the frost, sprinkling light on the spiders' invisible webs. It sent the shadows of high grasses onto the empty highway, and spread across the sleeping town, greening the tops of the tall pine trees. It lit the roof of the new Commission building and slipped down the sides, firing the windows and warming the sandstone to a rosy glow.

Tyler Waites, cycling south on Ashley Avenue, fingers chilly in his gloves, saw the burn and glow and let it warm him. As he came nearer, he slowed and stopped. Vandals had been there already. He rode closer until he could read their writing over the fiery copper-clad doors.

Deep down and under
Up to the sky
Shining and plunder
The well runs dry

Odd words for graffiti, and oddly-formed letters, hinting of Cyrillic or Greek. The paint had been carefully matched to the sandstone; the writing was like shadows on the wall. Tyler rode on, pedaling in the rhythm of the rhyme.

Ashley Avenue became a gravel road just outside the city limits, and then the road ended and he was riding on a dirt track into the woods. When he came to the fence, he leaned his bike against a tree and climbed over the sagging barbed wire, following a faint trail to the edge of the Punchbowl, an ancient sinkhole. He liked to be there just after sunrise, alone with the squirrels. He pulled a poncho from his day pack and spread it at the rim of the sinkhole to keep his pants dry.

Tyler was born in Opakulla, and his family had lived there until he was fifteen. As boys, he and his friends would slide down the Punchbowl on pieces of cardboard, then clamber back up through the brush and vines to slide down again. At dusk, chased by mosquitoes, they returned home scratched, bruised, and happy.

His sinkhole days had led Tyler to study geology, and in the end, the Punchbowl had brought him back to Opakulla. Though he went to college in Cambridge and grad school in Ann Arbor, he had never felt at home up north. The people he knew in those college towns were all alike. They all had the same opinions, and it made them smug and oblivious. He shared the opinions, but never without doubts, remembering all the people in Opakulla who would disagree with them.

Politics aside, the North was cold, and he could never get used to it. He loved the gentle winters and fierce summers of Florida. The wide peninsula drooped down from the continent, a world of its own. Its occupants thought they could stop the ocean from washing away its shores, the ground from collapsing beneath them. His dissertation on sinkhole formation had brought him offers from Berkeley and Princeton, but he had turned them down to come home to Opakulla University.

—•—

Now the ancient sinkhole was a state park. A wooden boardwalk led halfway around it to a flight of 230 stairs, all the way to the bottom. It was the only public access to the Punchbowl, but the Park Service allowed Tyler to go wherever he liked.

He sat huddled against the chill of the woods still empty of sunlight, his arms wrapped around his legs and his chin on his knees, gazing out across the sink. It had caved in a thousand years ago. Now it was a deep bowl full of trees, with bubbling springs trickling down the sides. Swampy tupelos grew next to sandhill pines, rattlesnake ferns in the deep shadows of chestnut oaks. Sitting on the rim, he felt like a monkey perched in a tree, with the sky down close on top of him.

It was almost 7:30 when Tyler stood up, shook the leaves out of his poncho, and walked back to the fence to retrieve his bike. When he arrived at Vernell's Breakfast Bar, Jared Coggins was already there. He and Vernell Potano were talking about her great grandson. Everybody knew about Curtis: he was the smartest boy in his class, but he couldn't stay out of trouble. So far, the creativity of his pranks had convinced the juvenile court to keep him out of detention, but the judge was running out of patience.

Jared sat at a table. Vernell was washing down the counter with a wet cloth, rubbing harder and harder as she talked.

"He's going to be the death of his mama, and he's only thirteen."

Tyler sat down with Jared, and Vernell brought his coffee.

"You going to have biscuits this morning, Tyler?"

"Yes, please."

"Well, just hold on a minute, and I'll whip some up fresh for you."

"Oh no, don't bother, I'll just have toast."

"No bother. Do it now or do it later." Vernell's had a rush around nine o'clock, old men who would sit around the rest of the morning until the lunch crowd drove them out.

"They're dedicating the new Commission building today. Are you going down to hear your cousin make a speech?" Tyler asked Jared.

Tyler had known Jared since they were boys together, hunting snakes in the Marsh to sell to the biology lab at fifty cents a head. But now, when they saw each other at Vernell's, Tyler struggled to make conversation. Jared was very shy and his discomfort was contagious. He had grown up in Opakulla, and had come back home as soon as he graduated from Georgia Tech. When HSI set up their southeastern headquarters in Opakulla, he took a job with their IT department. Working at HSI he should know plenty of people, but Tyler sometimes wondered if Jared had any friends besides Vernell and him. When he thought about it, the only other friend he himself had was Gerald Stone, and he didn't want any others. Maybe Jared didn't either.

"No. Marybeth isn't the mayor anymore. Now it's Randall Fairchild."

Vernell was back from the kitchen with Tyler's breakfast, biscuits, grits and scrambled eggs. Tyler stirred the eggs into the grits and poured hot sauce on top. Vernell gave him the same look she always did.

Tyler and Jared were silent for a few minutes, eating. Then Jared said, "I saw your boss, Dr. Stone, on the television last night."

"How did you like his speech?"

6

"It was a good speech, I guess." He seemed to be struggling with his mouth, gathering the nerve to say more. "Actually, I thought he sounded a little full of himself."

"Well, he's been leading that battle for two years, and you know, if it weren't for him, they never could have won against JJ Visions."

"I don't know, Tyler. What did they win? The owners will donate the swampy part of their land to the county, right up by the park boundary, but they couldn't have built on it anyway. Now they can build that whole big subdivision, and they get good publicity and a big tax break. Developers always win in Opakulla, and JJ Visions is going to destroy the Marsh."

"Rich folks give away a swamp and poor folks praise their name," said Vernell.

She was always saying things like that, as though she were the Voice of the Ancients. From anyone else, Tyler would have found it annoying. But Vernell was not like anyone else. He'd known her, only slightly, since he was a little boy. His father used to take him on a Saturday for a treat of Vernell's homemade peach cobbler with ice cream. Now she had to be in her eighties; her skin was wrinkled as a shelled pecan and she had lost most of her teeth. But she still stood tall and straight, in the long bright caftans she always wore.

"We don't know their name," said Jared.

"Sure we do," said Tyler. "The land is owned by that New York company. Wilson Trust Enterprises, or something like that. They're the ones who hired JJ Visions."

"But who are the people behind the Wilson Trust?"

"I don't really see what difference it makes."

He was disappointed. He was proud of what Gerald had done, and he had thought Jared would be impressed by Gerald's presentation to the Commission. Gerald Roderick Stone had courted Tyler to come to Opakulla University, though Tyler hadn't needed any persuading. Gerald was originally from Pennsylvania, but he had made his name in Opakulla; geologists all over the world knew his work in the underwater caves of Florida.

Two

The phone was already ringing as Marybeth reached her office in the new Commission building. She'd come in the back door, since they were putting up bleachers at the front. She rummaged through her purse, fumbled with her keys, lunged through the door and caught the phone mid-ring.

"Is this Commissioner Coggins?"

Who else would be answering my private line? "Yes it is."

"Commissioner Coggins, this is Willis Ames. I'm very sorry to bother you ma'am but we seem to be having a problem down here where we're setting up for the ceremony. I wonder if you could come down here ma'am. I tried to get Commissioner Fairchild, but he isn't here yet and when I tried him at home on his cell—I don't like to call the Commissioners at home, but this seems like kind of an emergency—anyway all I got was his voice mail. Commissioner Williams, his wife said he'd already left, and then you know Commissioner Lagrue, he's out of town because his cousin up in Folkston passed away and he's the only one left of the family to take care of the arrangements."

"Willis, it's okay. Why don't you tell me what the problem is."

"Well, Commissioner, it would really be better if I could get one of the men, it's not probably something a lady would know how to handle, but like I said...."

She knew he meant no harm.

"I'll be right down."

She put her purse in the deep bottom drawer of her desk and locked the door behind her. She took the stairs. The brand-new elevators were causing problems. A judge had been trapped in one last Wednesday, and all seven Commissioners had received a vitriolic memo about it the same morning. At this rate she was going to be losing a lot of weight without half trying. She could already feel the pull in her calves from her walk up.

She came out the back door and rounded the corner of the building. Everything seemed to be ready, the bleachers set up on either side of the fountain, the podium in place in front of the doors, with seven folding chairs lined up beside it, a broad white ribbon tied around the door handles. But behind the podium was a man on a ladder, scrubbing away at the wall with a long-handled brush, soapy water running down his arm. A little group of men was staring up at him. Willis broke from the group and came over to her.

"Commissioner Coggins, I don't know what to tell you. We've tried everything we can think of, and the contractor came over early to see what he could do, but somebody's gone and painted graffiti over the door, and we just can't get it off."

The worker was coming down off the ladder, and now she could see the writing above the doors. The stone was damp and dark from its washing, but the big curving letters were even darker.

She read the words silently, and then out loud. They gave her a little chill.

"I don't think you're going to be able to wash that off, Willis."

"Ma'am, I'm afraid you're right; we've already tried paint remover and muriatic acid. I think we're going to have to sandblast it. But there's no time for that now before the ceremony."

"I'm not even sure you're going to be able to blast it off."

"So what are we going to do?"

"I'll tell you what. See if you can find another flag and try hanging it down from the roof. We've still got almost an hour."

"There's that big flag over at the new industrial park. My uncle's in charge of grounds over there; I'll call him and see if we can borrow it."

"Good idea. That should take care of it for now."

Willis hurried off. The little group of men scattered and the worker took the ladder away.

Marybeth sat on the edge of the fountain, staring up at the letters. Why was she so certain those words wouldn't be blasted away? They seemed to be essential to the stone. Without them the building would vanish. As she stared, she heard them, not in any human voice, but in a voice of wind that filled the world around her. It pulsed in her blood, echoed off her bones. "Deep down and under…." Over and over it sang in her body, a song of sorrow, a song of warning. And then the voice left her as suddenly as it had taken her, and there she was sitting on the edge of the fountain, her hands still braced on the rough new concrete.

She'd never felt anything like it, except maybe that one night at the summer revival meeting when she was a girl. She looked around to see whether anyone had noticed her spell, but apparently it had lasted only a moment. The TV camera crew were just arriving in their truck. The workmen had finished setting up and had sat down for a smoke before returning to their jobs. She glanced warily at the words again, but this time they let her be.

By the time Randall and the other Commissioners arrived, Willis had rigged the flag up under the eaves of the roof. It covered the words perfectly, and the breeze flattened it against the sandstone. Marybeth thought it made a very nice touch, the Stars and Stripes spread up there above the doors. She stood up, dusted the crumbs of concrete off the back of her skirt, and took her seat with the others.

The turnout for the dedication ceremony was just about what she'd expected. Four homeless men, who'd found the new plaza as soon as the benches were installed, had been waked up by the work crews. They wandered over and took their places in the front row of bleachers. The city manager, the head of Buildings and Grounds, and the presidents of the Chamber of Commerce and the Junior League sat in front too, but at the other end. A few old people drifted from the café across Main Street, carrying containers of coffee. Jane Ellis brought her third-grade class to hear the speech, and let the kids climb to the very top row. Marybeth leaned over to Randall.

"I think this is as much of a crowd as you're going to get. You might as well get started."

—•—

Marybeth was probably only trying to be helpful, but her tone was irritating; it reminded Randall of his mother. He glanced at his watch, and deliberately let the second hand make another full circle before beginning.

"Ladies and gentlemen, I welcome you today to the Opakulla Community Plaza, for an auspicious moment in the history of our beloved town. Today we celebrate the fulfillment of a dream, a dream we see rising now before us…."

When he realized the building was behind him, he barely paused.

"…in sandstone and glass. This dream come true, this vision made real, is a symbol of so much that we in Opakulla hold dear."

—•—

Marybeth's mind wandered with the thin wisps of clouds sailing above the live oak in the middle of the plaza. Randall's voice was soothing, slightly gravelly, the voice of a classical music deejay. He didn't like her to call him a deejay. He was a radio announcer, he told her. She tried to remember, but really, classical or country, he was spinning records just the same, or whatever they did nowadays. Still, it was a wonderful voice for speeches, and she'd been happy to hand the mayor's gavel over to him in their semi-annual rotation. Now he could make the speeches and take the heat. She listened to his words in snatches.

"…symbolizes the spirit of cooperation…when the City Council and the County Commission agreed to consolidate… today that new government enters its new home…the cooperation of so many of our citizens…Opakulla University…the Chamber of Commerce…raising the money to build it…the builders of Opakulla worked overtime…."

But it wasn't the builders of Opakulla who got the big contracts, she thought. The fight over the general contract had been long and hard, but in the end the Commission had given it to a Miami firm.

"…a symbol of hope that we can fulfill our other dreams…generous gift from the Wilson Investment Trust…JJ Visions' new condominium development…expand our Marsh

Preserve…recreation for our youth, employment opportunities
….”

Oh Lord, now he was starting in with his goofy ideas: dirt
bike trails into the Marsh and an alligator farm for the restaurant
market. She could guarantee he wouldn't be seeing any spirit of
cooperation when he brought those to the Commission.

When he finished his speech, Randall waited a moment to
see whether anyone would applaud, and then took the shears out
from under the podium. Marybeth and the others lined up next
to him for the photographers. Willis had it perfectly timed. As
the ribbon fell away, water burst up from the fountain, rose from
the broad center pool and then leaped out in magical arcs to the
smaller pools around it. Back and forth, from pool to pool,
dancing around the bubbling column, shining strands of water
broke free and hung in the air a moment before they fell.
Marybeth could have watched it for hours.

But the people in the bleachers weren't looking at the
fountain. They were looking up over the doors, whispering to
each other, some of them pointing. She turned and saw that one
of the cords had slipped its knot. The flag hung by one corner,
swinging slowly beside the words on the wall. Now the letters
flashed and sparkled as if they were calling the sun.

“Can you explain the meaning of the words, Commissioner
Fairchild?”

Sam Jarvis, the anchorman from Sun TV News, had the
microphone in Randall's face. For the first time in his life,
Randall understood how it felt to be speechless. After a pause
that was far too long, he said simply, “No.”

“You mean you commissioned a poem that you can't
understand?” Sam was floundering too.

"We didn't commission anything; it's just there. I don't know where it came from. We'll wash it off, of course. It's a shame that someone would show such disrespect for our community on this special day."

—•—

The next morning it was on the front page of the *Opakulla Chronicle*, down at the bottom, with a picture of the Commissioners all lined up.

DEDICATION MARRED BY
MYSTERY VERSE

County officials yesterday were unable to explain the appearance of a mysterious poem on the new Commission building. The words were revealed when the flag fell down at the dedication ceremony for the building, which was built with $14.7 million in public and private funds. The poem read, "Deep down and under, up to the sky, shining and plunder, the well runs dry."

Mayor Randall Fairchild dismissed it as "meaningless doggerel," and promised that the writing, which he attributed to vandals, would be cleaned up immediately. Commissioner Marybeth Coggins, however, expressed doubts. "[The Department of] Buildings and Grounds tried to clean it off before the ceremony. It seems to be growing out of the building somehow."

Officials are further puzzled by the fact that the words do not show up on either video or still photography. A Chronicle photographer snapped close-up shots of the four-line verse, but the pictures revealed nothing but a blank wall. Sun TV news crews reported the same results on their video of the scene.

That morning Marybeth had attended a ground-breaking at the new medical school clinic. Sometimes it seemed as though her job was nothing but ceremonies and meetings. She had an appointment in an hour, on the same side of town, so it didn't make sense to go back to her office. Instead she went to Vernell's for coffee and cinnamon toast and a rare treat: Vernell came out from behind the counter with another cup of coffee and sat down with her.

"I never see you anymore except on the TV."

"I know. This job takes all my time; I hardly see Munro."

"How is he doing without you?"

"It's hard. We hired a helper, but you know how that is."

"I never tried it. Two hands is better than four when the second pair's all thumbs."

Marybeth had known Vernell since she was a baby. Her mother had been one of a little group of women, black and white, who met at Vernell's every week to keep track of things when the school board reluctantly began integrating the schools. Everyone but Vernell was shocked when the school board closed the black high school on the north side of town and built a new school on the south side. Vernell had seen it coming. The ladies called her prophetic, but "I know my history," said Vernell.

Now she wanted to hear about the words.

"Vernell, they're really strange. First time I saw them they wrapped me around and filled me up. They frightened me—they're trying to tell us something."

16

"You're right. Something's coming. Last night one of my ancestors spoke to me in a dream."

"Your great grandpa you told me about, from the black Seminoles?"

"That was my mother's people. My father came from the Timucua on Great Cypress Island."

"I thought they all got wiped out."

"No, still some of us around."

"So what did your ancestor say?"

"I can't tell you that. She is my spirit guide. Her words were only for me."

Marybeth knew that Vernell was a Christian, and very active in her church. She'd never mentioned this mystical stuff. But there had always been something about her, a shimmering of history, of age upon age stretching behind her, some sense that she was connected to other forces, forces that people called magic when they couldn't explain them.

The line between nature and magic had never been clear to Marybeth. She was surrounded by daily miracles, which scientists purported to understand. Caterpillar into butterfly, little brown seed into glorious flower, sunrise and sunset—she had to take it on faith that somebody somewhere could explain it. She certainly couldn't. She'd grown up with a Christian God and a modern education, so an evolving creation was an explanation that suited her, but all the other explanations seemed equally plausible.

Three

The office of JJ Visions, Inc. was in a small shopping center on the north side of town. Jasmine and her twin sister Jade never would have built anything like it themselves, a low strip of boxy stores and offices, not a tree or shrub in sight. The black asphalt parking lot was so hot that mirage puddles shimmered on summer afternoons. But with everybody moving to the south side, the rent was low, and Jade had grown used to the steady pounding of bass in the walls from the aerobics studio next door. Jasmine, who spent a lot less time in the office, always said it made her feel jumpy.

"Never mind, Jas, we'll be out of here soon. We can rent the fanciest office on the south side when Sunrise Terrace is finished."

"Hell, Jade, we won't need to rent. We can build a whole office park, plant willows around the retention pond, have a jogging path. The good old boys will be lining up for leases."

She couldn't sit still, she was pacing the room. Jade tipped a champagne bottle toward her glass, but Jasmine shook her head.

"I'll tell you what, let's take the day off and go to the woods. It was sweet of you to buy champagne, but wouldn't you rather get high and go hiking?"

Jade looked over her list. Now that the Commission had finally approved the development, they could get started, and she had thousands of things to do.

"Why not? We've waited four years; we can wait one more day. Just let me email Wilson Trust, tell them we're ready to go."

"I'll go over to the house and get the dope, meet you back here."

"Jasmine, you think I'm going hiking in this?"

Jade was wearing a gray tweed suit and black pumps. She handled the business side of JJ Visions; Jasmine was in charge of construction.

"Okay, we'll both go back to the house. We can stop at the Cheese Cellar and get a picnic."

They took the jeep, and Jasmine drove.

Jade and Jasmine O'Connell had arrived in Opakulla fourteen years ago in a Volkswagen bus with a canoe strapped on top. They'd gone down to the Keys for the Halloween party, and driving back north they decided to cut through the center of the state to see what there was to see. It was midday when they crossed the Missitucknee River; they would have called it a creek if it hadn't been for the sign. They pulled over and scouted along the trees for a way down to the water, and when they found a path, they hauled their canoe off the van. Slipping and sliding, they struggled down the bank and dropped the canoe in the water.

They paddled upstream for a couple of hours, and then turned around, letting the current carry them. Jade was in back, but where the river widened as it ran through the Marsh, there was little need for steering. The afternoon sun beat through to their bones. Leaves drifted past on secret currents to the river's edge, where they spun and tumbled in the water boiling over the cypress knees. Turtles, piled like rocks, basked on a branch dipping into the river. They passed a tree full of egrets, lit by the sun. Bird calls pierced the blue sky. Jade laid the paddle on her knees and let the river give them one bend, one bird, one turtle at a time. She didn't have to say anything. They both knew they were home.

Now Jade rested her elbow out the open window of the jeep, her head in her hand. The wind blew in her face as she watched the Marsh sweep by. There was their billboard, on the right-hand side of the road. They'd put the first one up almost four years ago and replaced it twice. It faded quickly in the rain and sun.

SUNRISE TERRACE CONDOMINIUMS
BY JJ VISIONS, INC.
"Building your dreams"
COMING SOON

But it hadn't come soon. The Department of Planning didn't like the site design. The county road department wanted a traffic impact study, but that required clearance from the state. The acting director of the State Department of Transportation told the Division of Roads that he wasn't authorized to commit any more resources until a permanent director was appointed. (The previous director had resigned after he was indicted for taking a consulting fee from an asphalt contractor.) The water management district was backlogged on drain and fill applications and wouldn't be able to get to it for eight months. Even the fire department got in on the act; they said they couldn't be responsible for fire protection that far out unless the Commission gave them another station in the southeast. Nineteen months after they submitted the development plan, JJ Visions appeared before the Commission for the public hearing on the proposed final approval. Five other developers were there to watch. So were the Sierra Club, the Defenders of the Environment, the Nature Conservancy, and the Friends of the Earth.

"Growth, progress, new jobs," sang the builders.

"Cypress trees and eagle's nests," the environmentalists chorused.

And so the Commission sent it back to staff for further consideration.

Two more years of waiting and wrangling, of grumbling from the Wilson Trust. It was JJ Visions' first big contract, and they'd never understood how it came their way. Until the call from Martin Wilson, they'd been surviving, but barely, on real estate commissions and remodeling. All the time, they were waiting for the big one. Finally, the manager of the Trust called them to New York for a meeting. Martin Wilson had no interest in inspecting the property: he only wanted to see a market analysis, site plans, and financial projections. Jade had the impression that he just wanted to get Wilson Trust's only Florida holding off his hands. She worked non-stop for three months, her proposal satisfied him, and then she struggled for the next four years not to let their big chance slip away. Martin Wilson summoned her to New York from time to time and hinted that maybe one of the big developers could get things moving a little faster.

—•—

Jasmine turned onto a dirt track about a mile past the billboard.

"We're here, Sis," she said softly.

"I thought we were going to the woods."

"I wanted to walk the land instead."

The land owned by Wilson Trust was 193 acres of the Marsh between the highway and the lake, right at the edge of the state park and the little strip the Trust had donated to the county. Down by the lake was wet cypress hammock; closer to the highway was mostly hardwood and pine. They pulled their wading boots from the back of the truck, and Jasmine grabbed her snake stick. She'd parked the truck as deep in as it would go, and they started into the woods.

Too faint to be a path, the trail was nothing more than a sense of extra welcome past a bush or under a branch. When even that was lost, Jade took over, finding an opening in the thick scrub, crushing small palmettos under foot, closing her eyes to plunge through wiry branches. Alone in the woods, Jasmine could be lost in five minutes, unless she carefully memorized every step and turn. But Jade seemed to have a compass in her feet, so that after an hour of crashing through brush and twisting past trees she could turn and point and say, "The truck's that way."

She was leading them toward Cypress Lake now. They stepped on crisp, dry leaves, and the ground underneath sank and sucked at their feet. The cypress trees stood thin and gloomy, but beyond them Jade could see faint light, and a great blue heron praying for bream, and she knew they were close to the water.

"When we've drained all the swampy patches, we'll just have the retention pond at the entrance, and the view from here of Cypress Lake. Most of those cypresses are on our land. We'll take them down, and we'll have that view forever," Jasmine said.

They sat on a branch leaning out over the lake and smoked the joint.

As they walked back through the swamp to the higher land where they would build, they began their dreaming.

"Can you see it, Jade? Now we're walking on the boardwalk that goes to the edge of the park."

"And over past that oak, that will be the cypress deck on unit four."

"At sunset they'll be watching the light fade, and the trees become black shadows."

"Jas, it's really going to happen this time; we're going to get it done. We're going to build it."

Jade was staring back through the trees, and Jasmine watched her face. Jade had aged a little. There was a frown line between her brows from too many meetings with bankers, bureaucrats, and politicians. Jasmine was proud of how Jade dealt with the world, but she liked it best when Jade took off her suits and put on her jeans and could just be herself. All these years of dreaming, of struggling together. Nobody knew Jade like Jasmine and nobody knew Jasmine like Jade.

Four

Two weeks after the building dedication, the mysterious writing was still there. It sparkled in the sunlight, glowed in the moonlight. In the rain, the letters were dark shadows on the wet wall. Willis had sent his crew over with a sand blaster, but the fine sand only wore down the stone around the letters, so that the words stood out more clearly. A stone carver came up from Miami to try his chisels. They broke. Willis was in despair. He called the head of Building and Grounds, who called Randall, who put the matter on the special agenda for the following week.

In the meantime, the words were beginning to attract attention. The wire services picked up the story from the *Opakulla Chronicle*. The television networks sent crews from New York, since the local cameramen apparently didn't know enough about filters to capture the image. The New Yorkers tried all the filters they had, even persuaded Misaki Optics to send them a prototype from Japan that wasn't going to be marketed for another four months. But still the wall looked empty when they ran the tape.

Without a picture, the networks soon lost interest. But it stayed in the local paper, and National Public Radio decided to do a feature on Wednesday Magazine. Randall couldn't believe his luck; the host of the show was going to interview him. If this had happened just a couple of weeks earlier, Marybeth would still be mayor of the Commission.

They had asked him to find a scientist who could explain the writing. He called the two professors who had consulted with Buildings and Grounds, but they were both out of town. There were no other materials scientists at the College of Engineering, and no one else was interested. He sat with the University Directory on his lap, running his finger down the list. Geology, they knew about stone. Maybe someone there could talk to her.

—•—

Every day when Tyler arrived at the department, Carol Willoughby was already at her desk. The faculty offices were in a long hall behind the department office, and she greeted everyone arriving. She looked so polished, like a picture in a magazine, but her face softened with her wide smile.

Carol claimed to remember him from when they were kids, but he thought she was just being kind. They'd been in the same class from kindergarten to third grade, but when her parents divorced, she changed schools. They went to the same middle school, but Tyler wasn't interested in girls then, and besides, she was part of the student government crowd, and probably didn't even know who he was. His friends were three math club members who liked to hang out at the Punchbowl and hunt snakes at the Marsh.

Even though he didn't have much to say to Carol, he liked seeing her there at the reception desk. But today she had stopped him as he passed by.

"Commissioner Fairchild called first thing this morning. He's looking for someone to talk to NPR about the writing on the wall."

"I don't know anything about that. Why would they call geology? I thought I saw in the paper they had someone from the engineering school working on the problem."

"He said he's tried engineering, and they're all at a conference or something. I got the impression it was really urgent."

She sounded distressed. Why should she care whether the radio station got their interview? She was so helpful to everybody, it made him want to help her out. So he agreed that if she couldn't find anyone else, he would talk to the reporter. Carol was obviously pleased, but he went down the hall to his office annoyed that he'd agreed to do it. He thought he had learned to say no long ago. Odd to see that pleading puppy look on Carol.

Tyler knew he was not an exciting speaker. When he read a paper at a conference, the coughing and yawning began unusually early. And that was when he knew what he was talking about, with a speech all prepared. What did he know about the writing? When he first saw it, he'd thought it was ordinary graffiti. He sat at his desk, fiddling with a pencil.

Gerald knocked and opened the door in one smooth motion.

"Good morning, Tyler."

Tyler cleared away some journals and offered him a chair.

"I understand you're going to be on *Wednesday Magazine* next week." His tone was jocular.

"Yes, and I'm sorry I said I'd do it. I don't know anything about the writing."

"Well, for heaven's sake, why did you agree?"

He seemed put out about something; in fact, his face was quite pink. His tweed jacket matched his salt and pepper hair and beard, and suddenly Tyler thought, *What's black and white and red all over?* and pictured Gerald pink and naked. His mind tossed up these junk thoughts like flotsam onto a beach. He hauled himself back to the subject at hand.

"It's so hard to say no to Carol, you know how she is. I had the feeling she had promised Randall Fairchild. And I guess she couldn't find anyone else."

"She should have asked me."

"Hey, do you want to do it? Do you know anything about the writing?"

"As much as you do, I'm sure."

"Gerald, please, feel free, you'd do a much better job than I would. It's more appropriate for you to do it anyway; you're the chairman."

Tyler couldn't understand his eagerness to be interviewed, but he knew Gerald would do a wonderful job if he could think of anything to say. Tyler was happy to turn it over to him.

Five

Randall stood in front of the full-length mirror in his bedroom, pulling yet another necktie out from under his collar. He tried a grey and navy stripe. If only he knew more about Adrienne Shelby. He had read an article about her several years ago in Airtime. She started her radio career in journalism school and moved to three cities before she got the job at NPR. Walked right in and they gave her a show, just like that, thirty minutes every Wednesday. It would never have happened to a man, thought Randall. The network was under pressure for not hiring enough women, so she had a real advantage. Randall had been trying to make a move at the same time, but none of the networks were saving any slots for him. He sent his resume to the public radio station in every city over 500,000 and didn't get even a nibble.

It was his last attempt to escape Opakulla. He had thought he was resigned to staying on here forever, but knew that he was hoping for something to come from this meeting with Adrienne Shelby. Of course, she was on the news side, but she probably had some pull with the arts people. He was skipping today's Commission meeting to devote his afternoon to her.

He looked critically at himself in the mirror. Unlike so many radio announcers, his appearance matched his voice. Tall, distinguished, square-jawed. The grey was coming in evenly all through his hair, giving him a perfect pepper and salt. And the little thinning in back was hardly noticeable.

The blue and grey stripe was too dull. He needed something more artistic. He finally settled on the hand-painted teal and burgundy.

Her plane was due in forty-five minutes. For the first time since he moved to Opakulla he blessed the dismal air service that would force her to spend the night. She would have a chance to hear his evening program after dinner and catch an hour of his morning show before he picked her up to take her to the airport.

Carefully, he hung all the ties on the rack in the closet. He made the bed and then, as a thought struck him, stripped it down and put on clean sheets. There had been no picture with the article he read, but she had been friendly on the phone. Of course, the odds were against anything like that, but you never know. Carol slipped into his mind, but he slipped her right back out again. Their relationship wasn't serious; they were really not well-suited. There was something vulgar about her. It was in her voice, a country-southern softness that made him think of sex at the most inappropriate times.

The flight from Atlanta was late. The flight from Atlanta was always late. Randall sat at the coffee bar. The coffee was charred from standing too long, so Estelle took his cup back and told him she would made a new pot. As he watched her retrieve the offending pot and retreat to the back with it, he heard a familiar voice behind him.

"Randall, I want to tell you, you did the right thing on that planning board appeal."

Oh God, it was Dick Westmeyer, president of First Southern. He'd called all the other bankers during Randall's campaign, and given $300 himself. Randall could have financed the campaign easily—he had invested in the stock market ever since high school—but he needed to prove he could get support. So now Dick considered himself Randall's advisor. At least this time he approved. Once he had stood over Randall in a restaurant, scolding like a father while the sauce congealed on Randall's snapper.

Sometimes Randall wondered how he had ended up as a Commissioner. The campaign was a nightmare of forced friendliness he thought he would never recover from and would certainly never repeat. He had run for office out of some dim notion that he could encourage the arts in Opakulla, but he spent most of his time tangled in endless wrangles about sewers and zoning variances. Now he understood that he had been an ideal candidate: handsome and articulate, with a beautiful speaking voice, and not a clue about the issues. The Chamber of Commerce rushed in to fill the void and managed to hold on to him during the campaign, but after a year in office he had started to have his own ideas. He had two years to go, and he knew he would never be elected again, even if he could bear another campaign, but he intended to leave a legacy. Opakulla was ready to grow, and he would see that it developed responsibly.

When the plane came in, Randall stood at the gate peering at the passengers as they came through the door. There was a woman in a tan wool suit, with shining black hair. But she wasn't looking for anyone to meet her; she walked directly toward the baggage claim. A fat, youngish woman in a gray dress with a well-draped scarf got off, but she was met by her husband. It wasn't until all the greeters found their passengers, and everyone had moved to the front of the terminal to get their baggage, that Randall noticed the woman in a khaki jacket that seemed to be made entirely of pockets. She wore hiking boots and knee-length shorts, carried a flight bag, and had a day-pack on her back.

"Mr. Fairchild?"

It was Adrienne Shelby's crisp, clean voice.

Why in God's name would she come to Opakulla dressed for a safari? It soon became painfully clear. After she interviewed him and the head of the Opakulla University geology department, she wanted to see the Marsh.

"What I want to do is tie the oracle into the spookiness of the Marsh. Do an intro on gators and Spanish moss and will o' the wisps, give it some local color."

How had she heard about the Marsh? She was going to turn this into some dreadful Old Southern Legends sideshow.

"Well, I'm not sure we're going to have time to go to the Marsh. I would have to change my clothes."

"Oh, I'd rather go by myself anyway. Get more of the feel of the place, and it's hard to write my script with someone else there; you know how it is. Actually, I've really been looking forward to seeing the Marsh; I'm quite a nature lover. In fact, I bought some of this gear just for the trip."

"But I've arranged a dinner for you. We have a rather nice little restaurant that two young women from California started last year, and there are a number of people I'd like you to meet."

He pulled a schedule out of his briefcase as if he thought it might persuade her. She read through it, looking suspiciously grave. Now her tone could only be described as kindly.

"You know, I get so much California cuisine in Washington. Do you think your friends would mind if we switched the dinner to some barbecue place? Then I could come straight from the Marsh and I wouldn't have to change. I didn't really bring clothes for a dinner party anyway."

31

He had no choice. He was relieved not to go to the Marsh himself; it was nothing but a lot of mud, snakes, and mosquitoes. He had thought they could spend the afternoon at the University Museum, which had an exhibit of eighteenth-century engravings on loan from the Canadian National Gallery. Now he'd be calling everyone to change the dinner plans, and she'd be mucking around in the Marsh. Serve her right if a snake dropped on her head.

If she planned to go off on her own, she would have to rent a car. Randall gave her directions to the University, the Commission building, and the Marsh. He had counted on getting to know her as he drove her around. Now it seemed unlikely that he'd have any real time alone with her.

—•—

Randall parked in his reserved space and walked around the Commission building to the plaza. It was a perfect winter day, the air crisp, almost chilly, and the sun hot. The bare dogwoods surrounding the plaza were as black and graceful as calligraphy against the pale blue sky. He sat on an empty bench and took off his jacket, folding it carefully over his knees. The sun warmed his shoulders. When he breathed deeply he could smell a faint flowery perfume.

He really should stop dreaming of major markets and settle in Opakulla. There was so much to do here. The fountain was just a beginning. He'd persuaded them to look beyond Florida and get proposals from artists all over the country. The winning proposal was from a German sculptor living in San Francisco. No one could deny that the fountain was a success. It had even been nominated for an NEA citation.

People in Opakulla weren't afraid of change, and they had visions of what a rich cultural life could be. The trouble was, a lot of them didn't realize the need for developing business too, as a way to support the arts. Now that the Sunrise Terrace issue was resolved, they were starting to mutter about his plans for the Marsh.

The Opakulla environmentalists were as fierce and numerous as Marsh alligators. They loved the Marsh, though he couldn't see why, but they didn't understand that the best way to protect it was to make sure it was economically viable. The alligator farm wouldn't even make a dent in the population; in fact, there would probably be more gators with careful management. And the dirt bike paths would only be at the very perimeter of the Marsh. People didn't realize what a serious problem there was with juvenile crime. Kids needed something to do besides hang out. He'd learned so much since he became a commissioner.

Maybe he should stay on here. He'd always felt temporary. Buying the condo would make a difference. He'd thought of buying before, but he could never find anything that suited him. Sunrise Terrace was just what he'd been looking for. He'd given JJ Visions a deposit on a three-bedroom end unit, in the building closest to the state park. The O'Connell sisters were certainly peculiar, but compared to their plans, the other developers were just putting up prefabs. He could picture the high white ceilings, the light filtering in through the trees. At last he would have a place to hang paintings, to display his collection of ivory carvings. The third bedroom would be his music room. The O'Connells had promised to modify the design with an acoustical engineer, hired at his expense.

He hadn't told Carol about the music room. She probably thought he'd chosen three bedrooms with her children in mind, but she hadn't said anything and neither had he. The vision of his new home didn't include two small children and a plump and harried woman who'd never even finished college. Somewhere in Opakulla, with all the new people coming in every year, he ought to be able to find a woman of some sophistication and flair.

"You ready to start?" Adrienne was standing in front of him. She'd left her bag and pack in the rental car, and had the microphone hooked up. She looked rumpled and sweaty.

"Well, of course. Let me show you around the plaza, and you can see the writing."

"I've seen the writing. Is it really true the letters can't be photographed? Must be some trick of the light. Let's run through the interview, and then we'll tape it. I want to get on to the Marsh."

She hurried him through his answers.

"All right, I've got the drift of it. Let's try to do this on the first taping."

She switched on the mike, tested, and turned some dials. Her voice became deeper, more gentle.

"I'm here in the Opakulla, Florida, community plaza in front of the new city-county Commission building, talking with Randall Fairchild, the Mayor of the Opakulla Commission. It's a beautiful day, warm as springtime, water from the new fountain is leaping to the breeze, and the famous words over the door seem to be lit by something more than the sun. Now, Mr. Fairchild, would you read the words for us, and tell us when they first appeared?"

When they had finished taping, Randall told Adrienne one more time how to find the Marsh. She agreed to let him pick her up at the hotel for dinner, because Pepper's Barbecue was hard to find. He went back to his office to make the phone calls. First, cancel the reservation at Monica's, then call the eight others. Most agreed, with some grumbling, to meet at Pepper's. He couldn't get hold of Lia or Don, but he left messages. They were vegetarians, so he was pretty sure they wouldn't show up.

—•—

Adrienne was waiting for him in the hotel lobby. Her boots were covered with mud, but she had changed into clean pants.

"You didn't tell me about the mosquitoes."

That explained the pink lumps on her face. She seemed cross and didn't want to talk about her walk in the Marsh.

They were the last to arrive at Pepper's. Randall was right about Lia and Don, but everyone else had shown up. Ted was director of the community theater. He was there with his wife Lucille, who was surprisingly mousey. Felicia and Howard owned a frame shop. David and Walter had a nursery and landscaping business; they had been together for years. There were two pitchers of beer on the table already, and one of them was almost empty.

There was a sticky spot on the table under Randall's arm.

"Would you mind cleaning that off, please?"

"I don't mind at all, honey," and the waitress wiped off the table with a dirty, wet cloth. "Can I get you all glasses?"

Adrienne asked her what kind of beer they had, and she named three.

"You don't have any imported beer?"

"Just Lowenbrau."

"Never mind, I'll just share the pitcher."

Adrienne ordered the Pepper's combo: ribs, sliced pork, and chicken, with fries, beans, and Texas toast.

"I think you may find that's too much for you," said Randall.

"Oh, you'd be surprised at how I eat."

Randall was surprised too at how she drank. She was already on her third glass of beer when the food came, and Pepper's was famous for fast service. Her springs uncoiled a bit as she drank. She went around the table, asking everybody what they did. Lucille murmured, "Oh, well, I have two children."

"Isn't that lovely. I bet they keep you busy."

When the food came, she turned her attention to Randall, and smiled encouragingly as he told her about "Musical Notes," his evening talk and music show which was carried by three other NPR stations in Florida. She ate steadily as she listened.

—•—

After the clamor of Pepper's, the car was very quiet. He could hear Adrienne breathing. The night was chilly, with stars bright against the black sky. As they drove back to the south side of town, she suddenly pulled the lever and let the back of her seat down. He looked over, startled. Her legs stretched straight in front of her and her arms dangled back over her head.

"I feel wonderful. What a gorgeous night."

It was a voice for an audience of one. Randall was taken aback. He hadn't thought of this since he first encountered her at the airport. He took another look. It was hard to tell what kind of figure she had under all those pockets. From the neck up she was all right—brown eyes, brown hair, small nose, wide mouth—surprisingly pretty for a radio announcer. The little hollow just below the smooth curve of her throat was positively appealing.

It never occurred to Randall that he might ignore the opportunity. He wasn't one for cruising bars or coming on to a woman at a party just because she was unattached. But as long

36

as his equipment was in good working order, there was no reason to pass up an invitation.

He began to calculate his first move. Should he invite her to his place? He remembered the clean sheets on his bed. But she was ahead of him.

"It's too early to call it a night. Why don't you come up to my room for a drink when we get back to the hotel?"

In the room she was brisk and efficient. She pulled a bottle of vodka out of her overnight bag.

"Ice and soda are down the hall. I'm going to change."

She was in the bathroom when he came back. He turned off the center light but left the bedside lamp on. He took off his jacket and hung it in the closet, started to take off his tie but decided just to loosen it. He began to feel nervous and picked up his drink. Then the door opened and she came out.

What the khaki pockets had hidden, a red nightgown revealed. There was lace over her breasts, translucent silk below.

"You look very beautiful."

"Thank you. Pour me a drink too, please."

She sat in an armchair and watched him as he undressed. He almost lost his balance removing his pants. This wasn't going well. He was shrinking under her gaze. If he could somehow get over to the bed without turning to face her. No, he would leave his briefs on, go over to her, get things started. He was sure propinquity would do the trick.

It did, and quickly. Her skin was warm and soft, and she smelled delicious. She pulled down her gown so he could reach her breasts. It fell the rest of the way as they moved to the bed. She was in rather a hurry, and he was a little disconcerted by her instructions on position and pace, but together they got the job done. She lay with her eyes closed, giving him a chance to stare at her unobserved. She was very beautiful, with none of the stretching and sagging of Carol. Still, he had to admit, making love to Carol was much more exciting. With Adrienne it had been like sharing a sneeze. He reached over and began stroking her shoulder. She opened her eyes.

"Well. That was very nice. I guess it's about time for you to go."

"Oh, now, I don't have to leave."

He ran his hand down on to her breast.

"That's nice of you, but I'm really kind of tired."

"Why don't we sleep awhile?"

"I don't sleep well with someone I don't know. I think you'd better get dressed."

It was a long drive home.

—•—

The next morning the sky was bleak, with a fine chilly mist. Randall decided to treat himself to a big hot breakfast. He'd heard people talking about Vernell's, and he decided to give it a try.

He parked in the dirt lot and sat a moment, looking dubiously at the small, windowless cinder block building. No cars in the lot, no sign, just "Vernell's Breakfast Bar" painted neatly over the green door. He'd look inside, and go somewhere else if it didn't suit him.

Inside, despite the lack of windows, the light was clear and bright with the freshness of dawn. A counter with six stools. Six booths and six wooden tables. All were empty.

"Good morning. You can sit anywhere you like." A deep, rich voice. He turned, and a tall black woman stood by a rocking chair in the corner. She wore an orange batik caftan with red and yellow birds flying up from hem to shoulder. Her hands were gnarled, her face deeply-lined; a glossy wig curled in a bob around her face.

He chose a booth near the door and looked at the menu. Eggs sunny side up, sausage, potatoes and a biscuit, juice, coffee—that should restore him. Vernell brought the coffee, and he settled back in the corner of the booth and examined the mural across the room, a tangle of cypress trees, beautifully rendered. Even the finest artist couldn't make the Florida landscape interesting, though the two eagles soaring above the tallest tree were a nice touch.

He didn't hear a car, but the door opened and a youngish man with a green backpack came in and sat at a table near the counter.

"Good morning, Vernell. Where's Jared?"

"You're early. I'm not looking for him for a while."

She brought him coffee and refilled Randall's cup, then returned to the kitchen. When she emerged again with Randall's breakfast, she brought a plate of eggs, grits, and a biscuit for the other customer, though Randall hadn't heard him order. Then she sat back down and began rocking.

"Don't know if that's my chair creaking or my bones."

"I guess this weather's rough on arthritis."

"Rougher on me."

"Can't the doctor give you something for that?"

"How am I going to see a doctor, Tyler? I'm still paying for that doctor who let my husband die ten years ago. No, I just take my powders and they help sometimes."

The door opened and a lanky man with greasy black hair came in. He kept his eyes down as he joined Tyler, and never looked at Randall.

"Mind if I sit down?" he murmured, and waited for Tyler's nod.

"Vernell, is it OK if I turn on the radio?" Tyler asked. "Gerald Stone was being interviewed yesterday, and I think they should be airing it pretty soon."

"Help yourself."

They listened in silence to the end of the headlines and then there was Adrienne Shelby talking about Opakulla. Randall felt his face flush, but none of them were watching him. Vernell stopped rocking to listen.

"The people here in Opakulla have grown up with the Marsh at their doorstep. The deep gloom of the cypress swamps, the hazy ghosts who bubble up out of the mud, the alligators, like survivors from prehistory, crawling through the wet grasses, are for them as ordinary as the daily paper. They gouge out the heart of the tall palm tree, and call it swamp cabbage. They make clocks and coffee tables out of the cypress. There's talk of herding the alligators into a big floating corral and harvesting their skins. But four weeks ago, the citizens of Opakulla met a mystery they couldn't explain."

It was her usual style. Randall suspected she was an aspiring novelist. He was next.

She had edited his ten minutes down to two sentences about their attempts to clean the writing off the wall. Tyler's companion glanced at him and quickly looked away.

Now Professor Stone spoke.

"I have not examined it myself, of course, but fundamentally we are talking about a change in the stone, apparently caused by moisture. In other words, the water flowing into the stone carried some kind of hardening substance. It also discolored the stone so as to form the words."

It was nothing new; it was just what the engineers had said in the *Opakulla Chronicle*. Of course, Adrienne was addressing a national audience; they hadn't heard any of this before.

Randall finished his breakfast and paid at the counter. He wouldn't come back here. The food was fine, and the place was clean enough. It was almost attractive, with that clever lighting that mimicked the dawn. But something about Vernell made him uneasy. She seemed already to have taken his measure and found him wanting.

—•—

When they heard his car pull away Jared said, "That was the Mayor, Randall Fairchild."

"You mean the guy who just left—he was the one on the radio? He didn't have much to say."

"Neither did that friend of yours, that professor."

"I know. Of course, he didn't have much time to prepare."

Tyler was disappointed in Gerald's remarks. Still, he didn't have any better explanation. He'd happily turned the interview over to Gerald, but no one seemed to be able to tackle the question of how the words were formed. Maybe it was time to call the religion department and ask about miracles.

"Mighty smart water, you ask me," Vernell said.

Jared spoke softly. "They say a thousand chimpanzees with typewriters could have written Shakespeare."

Six

When he left Vernell's, Tyler headed to the Marsh. The head ranger had told him that something odd was happening at Cypress Lake, and he wanted to take a look. He had his own route to the lake, from the southwestern edge. It would be much quicker to go in from the north, and his way was a long hike, but it took him through some of the prettiest parts of the Marsh. Two hours of walking, in the damp air under the trees, the warmth of the sunlight on the grasslands, took him to the tip of Cypress Lake, where the fragrant ladies' tresses were blooming among the cypress.

Hot from the long walk, he took off his sweater and sat in the shade. Though he had found a dry hummock to sit on, the leaf mold beneath his bottom was damp. Rest settled in through his body. The din of his footsteps, his pulse, his breathing, were quiet now, and he could hear the birds again.

Cypress Lake was shaped like an alligator with its mouth wide open, and Tyler was sitting right at the edge of a nostril. In the middle of the alligator's upper jaw, a dozen turtles lay in the sun on a branch that had fallen into the lake. Usually the duckweed covered the still water like a blanket, but today a current was running under the surface. Tyler tried to follow the

42

movement, but his gaze drifted with the tiny round leaves and lost focus. He found a stick on the ground beside him and threw it onto the water. The splash sent the duckweed trembling in rings, and three turtles dropped into the lake.

When all was quiet again, he watched the stick. It drifted in a wide circle, snagging itself for a moment on a water lettuce leaf, twisting away, floating on, floating as if it had all the time in the world to take its slow tour. Now he could see that the duckweed was moving in the same slow drift, counter clockwise, the circling dance broken at the bank, but smooth in the center of the water, so slow that a dead leaf lying on the duckweed traveled only a few feet in a minute. There was no denying the movement, no doubting the cause. Clearly, the lake was draining.

The words from the wall returned to him, *The well runs dry.* He'd thought it was vandalism; but how could vandals have known what was happening at Cypress Lake? For years Tyler had studied geology, the stories in rocks and soil of great changes in the earth. Now he sat perfectly still, watching a lake disappear.

It Begins

In a month the water had all drained away, and Cypress Lake was more like an alligator than ever, dark green and brown and black, the muck drying rapidly in the sunny cold of January. The trees on the bank were left high and dry, and the giants of Great Cypress Island stretched their roots in search of moisture. Slowly the turtles crawled away across the Marsh. The cottonmouths followed, and hung in smaller cypresses at Red Pond, hypnotized by their own reflections swinging in the murky water. The fish, trapped as the lake shrank, crowded together, and herons and ospreys and wood storks came from all over the Marsh to feed. Now, on the drying lake bed, a few dead fish remained for the turkey buzzards, and the mud was cracking in the sun.

The sinkhole began on New Year's Day; only two slugs saw the first crumbling of the mud. Just seventeen of their species remained on earth, all living in the Marsh. Had scientists ever discovered them, they would have been called endangered. The pair dangled from a slender string of slime, hanging from a bush near the edge of the lake bed, twined around each other, their airy love unhindered by surfaces. And below them a tiny hole opened in the ground, a hole that grew deeper and wider by the minute, the dry mud flaking and falling into it, until the edge of the hole reached the roots of the wax myrtle shrub where they were hanging. The bush shifted and fell, and the string of mucous broke. The slugs remained twined in the dried mud, writhing and shriveling as the hot sand buried them.

Seven

Tyler returned to the Marsh as often as he could. Cypress Lake had disappeared so quickly, and now he stood astonished at the edge of a deep round hole in the lake bed, thirty feet across. It was littered with rubble: crusts of dried mud, broken bushes and branches, whole trees fallen with their roots in the air. As he watched, a small slide began on the far side of the hole, then stopped as suddenly as it had begun. A few feet from him a chunk of mud broke off and tumbled down to the bottom. The ground was still sinking. He stepped back from the edge.

Two years before, at a conference in Krakow on sinkholes, Tyler had heard Dr. Stanislau Brezhnev describe the beginning of the Brezhnev sink. Stanislau spoke with awe of watching the deep hole forming in the dark pine forests. He didn't mention the mess and the rubble. It was hard to believe this crater would ever be filled with trees and flowing streams.

Tyler had to share this. Gerald had been back from winter break four days, but they hadn't seen each other. Tyler called him and they agreed to meet at The Cue, the pool bar in the center of town, where they wouldn't be surrounded by students.

They sat by the window, away from the pool tables. Four men were playing today, as well as a heavy-hipped woman in tight yellow polyester pants who had placed second in last year's tournament. Except for their exclamations and the click of the balls, the bar was quiet.

"There's a new sinkhole at the Marsh."

"You don't say. Well, that must be fascinating." Gerald was tamping his pipe. He wore full academic regalia: pipe, tweed, elbow patches, and all. It was unusual attire in the geology department, where most of the faculty wore jeans and t-shirts.

"I just found it today. It's thirty feet across already and it hadn't even started the last time I was there."

"Still active?"

"Seems to be, though I didn't see any activity while I was there except for some minor slides."

Gerald wanted to hear all about it: dimensions, soil, fluvial activity.

"Have you told anybody about it?"

"It's just happened."

"The rangers don't know?"

"I wouldn't think so."

"You need to get out there and get photographs, write something up quickly, before other people come along. It sounds like it's going to be a big one. This is your sinkhole, Waites. It could be as significant as the Punchbowl, or Old Cutler. They'll name it for you."

"Waites Sink? That doesn't sound right. Missitucknee Sink. Or Great Cypress Sink."

"Why Great Cypress?"

"Well, it's very close to Great Cypress Island, right at the edge of where the lake used to be."

"What do you mean used to be?"

"Oh my God, Gerald, that's right. I haven't told you about the lake draining. You know, I never thought I would see changes like these in my lifetime, much less in two months."

Gerald's eyes were narrowed, as they always were when he sucked on his pipe. He sat perfectly still for a moment.

"You say the lake has drained?"

"It's nothing but dried mud now."

"Why didn't you get hold of me?"

"Why would I do that?"

"For God's sake, Waites, what do you think this does to the Wilson Trust development? Have you forgotten how long it took me to negotiate that whole deal?"

Tyler certainly hadn't forgotten. He remembered the night Gerald had decided to step into the fight over JJ Visions' development proposal. In the ferocity of the battle to protect the Marsh, the environmentalists had turned on each other. The president of the Sierra Club resigned from Friends of the Earth after they accused her of selling out. Fourteen members of the Nature Conservancy threatened to sue the Defenders of the Environment.

Tyler had been about to go home after a long, disheartening afternoon of grading exams when he saw a light in Gerald's office. He knocked and went in to find Gerald surrounded by clippings from the *Opakulla Chronicle*, head in his hands. Gerald looked up. His face was drawn and tired. Tyler thought he had been crying.

"We're tearing each other to pieces and in the end the developers are going to have their way. If we can't work together any better than this, we'll end up with the whole marsh drained and paved."

Tyler had persuaded him to go out for a beer. He listened as Gerald rambled on about old friends turned enemies, new skirmishes in old wars, buried grudges dug up, still breathing. Tyler was amazed. Gerald knew the history of every member of every group. Tyler had never paid any attention to local politics. He just assumed developers controlled the politicians. He studied the earth because he loved it and knew it was dying.

Still, he found himself urging Gerald to get involved.

"You know, Gerald, you could make a difference. They all respect you. They need a new leader to bring them together."

After another beer, Gerald had promised to think about it. And the next week he called the leaders of every environmental group in town to a meeting at his house. It took four meetings to weld them into a coalition, Friends of the Marsh, and then a year and a half for them to negotiate a compromise with JJ Visions, Inc. Every time Gerald used the word compromise, the coalition threatened to shatter, but they kept coming back because JJ Visions had the law on its side. The coalition could delay them and play games with them and make them wish they'd never heard of Opakulla, but in the end they'd be building in the Marsh.

Gerald had been exhausted but proud when he and Jade finally were able to present their agreement to the Commission. Friends of the Marsh would drop their opposition; in exchange the Wilson Trust would give the county thirty-four acres of wet cypress hammock by the lake for a park, adjoining the Missitucknee Marsh State Park.

Now Gerald asked Tyler, "What do you think this does to the new county park?"

"I guess it won't be much of a park without the lake, will it? I wonder if JJ Visions will still want to build. They don't have a lake view to sell anymore."

"What about the sink?"

"Oh, it's nowhere near their land, it's on the north edge of the lake. But there are a couple of smaller ones too. You know, if they wait a couple of hundred years, they'll have a beautiful sinkhole park. They can run tours."

"It's obvious that you don't understand the significance of this. We invested a great deal of time and effort into working out an arrangement that will suit everybody. Now the county park is virtually useless."

Useless to whom? Tyler was puzzled. The point of the park, he thought, was simply to protect the swamp. Surely Gerald hadn't thought people were going to go walking through the muck to see Cypress Lake. There was a nature trail on the other shore and the rangers said hardly anyone ever went there.

"I have to call Jade O'Connell and tell her what's going on. She'll want to get out to the site."

Gerald was looking around for the waitress, emptying his pipe into the ashtray. He was suddenly all business. He'd turned off his excitement as if geology were a little boys' game.

"Shall I drop you at school or your place?"

"My bike's at the office. You'd better leave me there."

—•—

Jade agreed to meet Gerald at the Marsh the next day. He hadn't seen her since the day they presented their agreement to the Commission, and he was looking forward to it. Through the long negotiations he had sometimes felt she was his only ally against the forces of confusion. He could talk to her more easily than to all the factions he was trying to hold together, who watched him suspiciously, waiting for him to make one false move.

She'd teased him about his troubles. Once she sent him a card. On the front was a massive live oak, drawn with crayons, gray and brown and green. Hanging from its branches like moss, or monkeys, were tiny penciled people, wearing badges and waving signs. Inside she had written a verse:

Defenders, Friends, and Enemies
Are all in disarray,
And every holier-than-thou
Resolves to have his say.
Each bird and bug and creepy-crawl
An advocate has he:
You'll let us build our condos
But we mustn't touch a tree.
And you and I will argue on
Till all the seas run dry.
We'll still be squabbling when we build
Our mansions in the sky.

—•—

Jade's truck was parked at the beginning of a fire road. Gerald pulled his car in beside it and got out. Jade stepped out from behind an oak.

"Hey."

He'd always seen her in suits, square and solid. Today she was in jeans and a sweater. She wore no makeup. It was a warm day for January and her face was already pink and sweaty. A beautiful smile, and all her movements loose and easy.

"You look wonderful."

It made him happy to see her, like finding an old friend. They got in the truck and bumped along the road. Gerald inspected the clutter in the cab. A book on bass fishing in Florida, and the collected poems of Emily Dickinson. A yellow Styrofoam hamburger container, a receipt from Food King, an old postcard with an alligator about to bite the bottom of a blonde woman in a bikini. A small plastic Betty Boop, Mardi Gras beads, and a ball point pen on a chain hung from the rear-view mirror.

"Excuse the mess. This is really my sister's truck."

"How is your sister?"

"Till your call she was happy as a clam, buying and hiring, dickering with the subs. She would have been here today but she wasn't feeling well."

He'd met Jasmine just once, when Jade's car was in the shop and Jasmine came to pick her up from a meeting. Her crinkly red hair was long and loose. She wore jeans and sandals, and small gold hoops in her ears. She was like a wholesome Janis Joplin, smelling of sunshine and clean lumber instead of Southern Comfort. Meeting her he was struck by the oddest sense that Jasmine was the true Jade, the one he'd seen only in glimpses, the one who sent him the card and made jokes about the bankers.

He found himself intensely curious but didn't know if he was curious about Jasmine or Jade. He had invited Jade home for dinner a few times, and urged her to bring her sister, but she had always made excuses.

The truck bounced along the fire road and turned onto a narrower track, nothing but two sandy ruts through the brown grass. This dry winter followed a second dry summer. Gerald wondered if the lake had gone dry because of the drought.

The sun shone full in their faces. They were driving past an open field ringed by small red turkey oaks and green palmetto, with a tall sabal palm rising in the middle, topped by a sudden mop of fronds against the fierce blue sky. Then they were in the shade again, and the air that had been dry and dusty in his nostrils was now damp with leaf mold.

Jade stopped the truck and they got out. It was a short walk through the trees to the lake. When they came out in the clearing, he was astonished. It was as Tyler had said, of course. The water was gone. The lake looked so much larger when it was empty. Only the very center was still black and damp; the rest was dry, cracked mud, littered with withered water grasses. The big sink wasn't visible yet, and they began walking up the lake bed along the gator's tail.

Gerald felt a hesitation in the soles of his feet. He was reluctant to step where once the reflected sky had spread beneath the giant cypresses. They had to pick their way over the dips and rises that had been hidden by the water, the cracks in the dry ground. The sun pouring down raised the stench of rotten grasses and dead fish.

They had walked twenty minutes when they saw the first sign of the hole, a massive ball of roots sticking up in the air. They walked to the edge and looked down. For a moment, Gerald was a geologist again, gazing with wonder into this deep raw hole.

"I think this is bigger than thirty feet, Gerald."

"Tyler Waites measured it, but I believe it's still growing."

Just then, the center of the hole dropped slightly, and all around the edge the slides began.

"My God. It's beautiful."

"Jade. You're supposed to be building here."

"I know, but I've never seen anything like this. It makes me want to roll down into it, I've got to bring Jasmine out to see it."

"Watch out, you'll go down the hole and never be heard from again."

"Like the rabbit hole. Maybe Wonderland is underneath."

"Nothing but crushed limestone and more rubble."

"Let's walk around it."

"Okay, but you'd better keep away from the edge."

Gerald's impulse was to take Jade's elbow to guide her, but he held back. He sensed she wouldn't like it, and obviously she could pick her way through the roots and ruts perfectly well on her own. As they walked, he explained the formation of sinkholes as best he understood it, though he realized he was rusty, and he had plenty of questions that Tyler could have answered. But Jade listened with gratifying interest.

"We're a good way from the boundary of the land. Can you tell how much bigger it's going to get?"

"Oh, I can't imagine it's going to grow much larger. You may get a little more crumbling at the edge. Usually these collapse sinks are pretty quick; everything falls in at once. I believe this one is already as big as any in this area, except for the Punchbowl."

"Well, it's a shame to lose the lake view, but we've re-drawn the plans to face south, so the buildings are looking out over the rest of the Marsh, away from the park. It shouldn't affect the price. This is such a beautiful area anyway, and all the fuss has generated a lot of interest. We've got five buyers already."

JJ Visions would proceed with the development. Gerald hadn't realized how tense he was until Jade's words reassured him. It wasn't the negotiations, all the time he'd spent. Only his wife Helen knew what Sunrise Terrace meant to him, and the truth about the Wilson Trust.

Eight

Soon the curious were taking the long hike out to Cypress Lake to see the earth swallow itself. In the lake bed, and all around it, new sinks formed, and then the land between them collapsed, forming one big hole. It grew steadily, several feet a day, and as it grew, the news spread. Jade flew to New York to confer with Martin Wilson, and Gerald called a meeting of Friends of the Marsh to explain the loss of the county park.

Randall had taken a special tour of the site with the park rangers, and he was happy to discuss the phenomenon at the Harroways' party. It was eight o'clock, and the guests were milling around in the living room and out on the terrace, lit with clay oil lamps Lucille had picked up in Guatemala. An afternoon storm had left the air damp, filled with the scent of wet leaves; the sky was still rumbling and flickering. Randall stood in the center of a small group, with Carol Willoughby at his side, describing the draining of the lake.

"Quite suddenly, like Ars Poetica."

"Arse what?" asked Carol.

"Ars Poetica. It's a poem by Archibald MacLeish." He was ashamed of his tone, but vulgarity offended him, and Carol knew it.

He could tell she was getting bored, and he was beginning to be sorry he had brought her. He usually went out alone. In his position his social life was really more a matter of business than pleasure. Besides, he went out several nights a week, and she couldn't afford babysitters that often.

He didn't want anyone to consider them a couple, though tonight she looked very pretty, and she got along well with these people. There was real warmth in Lucille's greeting to her, and he had seen her deep in conversation with Lydia Framingham and her cousin. But then she came and joined him, and it wasn't ten minutes after he started explaining the sinkhole that she had to go and embarrass him like that. He'd seen Ted and Lucille exchange a glance at her ignorance, and smile. He resumed his discussion of the sinkhole, but people seemed to have lost interest.

They left the party shortly after, and he drove north toward her house.

"I was going to spend the night at your place," she said.

"Oh, sorry, I forgot. You know, I'm rather tired. Why don't we make it some other night?"

"You forgot. Don't you know what I had to go through to get an all-night sitter?"

"Yes, I do. You told me."

"So now what? I go home and kick her out of my bed? Or maybe I can sleep on the couch."

"I can just take her home when I drop you off."

"She's there with her baby, Randall. We traded, remember, and she's counting on leaving Jason with me next weekend."

"Well then, you can stay at my place if you want."

"Don't do me any favors."

But he turned and drove to his apartment.

—•—

Carol stood stiffly by the sofa, trying not to cry. She had looked forward to a rare night together. Now her body wouldn't move right, her joints felt stiff and awkward and she didn't want him to touch her. He was in the kitchen, mixing drinks and whistling one of his pretentious little tunes. She thought it was Mozart, but she was damned if she'd ask and let him correct her. He came out from the kitchen with two drinks in his hand.

"Why don't you sit down?"

She sat, not on the couch, but in his favorite armchair. She suddenly realized how tired she was and wished she had just told him to take her home.

She knew he was trying to figure out how to get her to move to the couch. The room was so clean and bare, so uncomfortable; not a place where she could kick off her shoes and put her feet up on the coffee table. It was a glass coffee table, with nothing on it but a soapstone carving of a whale and a book of abstract photographs. His elegant apartment wasn't nearly as nice as her shabby place on the north side. There was no life in it.

Her chair was facing the painting she hated. It was depressing, a jagged tangle of edges and lines in mustard and brown. Randall said it was by an important new artist who had already been in two group shows in New York. He could never simply like something. It always had to be by a rising young artist from Rhode Island, or the generally acknowledged best performance of the E flat major.

"Generally acknowledged by who?" she had asked him once, when she was feeling fed up.

"By whom," he had snapped at her.

He looked lost if a subject came along that he couldn't express a view on. His opinions, his clothes, his wine, always had to be correct. Even his messes looked arranged. On the table in the entryway were a hand painted silk tie, the New York Times Book Review, and an airmail letter from Barcelona.

She knew he was reluctant to take her to parties with what she always thought of with a smile as "the best people" of Opakulla, but she got on fine with all of them, the men and the women both. In fact, she probably got along with them better than Randall. She'd gone to school with a lot of them, or with their children, and all through high school she used to babysit for the Harroways.

Poor Randall was always trying to prove himself. He could never have a real conversation, but stood looking stranded with a drink in his hand until the talk came around to something he knew a lot about, and then he would start on one of his lectures. He had gone on so long about the new sinkhole that she had glanced at her watch to time him, and he'd still been holding forth five minutes after that, when she just couldn't stand it any longer and broke in with that crack she knew would embarrass him. She picked up the whale and began fondling it, cool and heavy in her palm. She held it up to her cheek and closed her eyes a moment to shut him out.

Carol had been going out with Randall for a little more than a year. When they met, she was instantly attracted to him and the world he moved in. She admired the ease of that world, an ease created by something so simple, and for her so unattainable: money.

She spent far too much time thinking about money. Every month she paid some bills on time and tried not to pay any bill late two months in a row. Her child support came so erratically that she had long ago decided to treat it as a bonus. She tried to put it into a savings account for the kids' college, but whenever the check came, something would happen, so usually she spent it before it ever reached the bank, on car repairs or at the emergency room. The savings account had only $310 in it, and she knew that even in ten years, when Robin was ready for college, it wouldn't make much difference. But as long as she had it, it meant she hadn't given up.

She had a secret plan to go to college herself at the same time as the kids. She had a fantasy of Robin's graduation, when her daughter's baby face would look across the stage to see her mother in a cap and gown, accepting her own diploma. Of course, it wouldn't be a surprise, the kids would know if she went back to college, but that was how she always pictured it. She had taken two night courses, but the babysitting cost too much, and every night she was home, she had to study. The kids were starting to get whiny and fight a lot.

—•—

Randall sat on the couch, wondering how he was going to get Carol to come sit next to him. He had forgiven her for her tasteless remark. She looked so self-contained over there in that armchair. Her skirt had ridden up just a little to show her big thighs. Carol could never be elegant, she was too short and chunky, but her body was round and solid. Nothing quivered when she walked, and he liked the firmness in his hands, the weight in his arms.

He had a vision of what it would be like if she lived there—she would be sitting in that chair, reading, and he would lie back on the couch, listening to music, and after a while she would come over and sit on the edge of the couch and take his hand. But of course, it wouldn't be like that with the two kids running around, and she'd probably want to rearrange the furniture.

She was waiting for him to say something. He stood up and went over to her, began rubbing her shoulders. He felt her relax under his fingers, and he leaned over and whispered,

"I guess I could let you spend the night."

Oh damn, she tensed again immediately, and here it came, no way to stop it.

"You don't even bother to think about my life, what I have to go through just to get an evening out with you and your so superior friends."

And that brought back vividly her rude joke and the smiles of Ted and Lucille.

"They're certainly superior to the sort of vulgarity you displayed tonight. You embarrassed me."

"You deserved to be embarrassed, Randall, going on and on like that about the sinkhole. It sounded like a goddamned lecture. Couldn't you see people were getting bored?"

"You were the only one getting bored, Carol. Everyone else was interested in learning something new."

"You know so much, don't you, with your college education and your perfect little life. Well you and none of your rich friends either know how to raise two kids on thirty thousand a year. Take me home. I don't have time for you."

—•—

The drive home was grim, of course. As Carol got out of the car, she said nothing but goodnight. It was a wonderful relief to be home. All the lights were off, and the bedroom doors were closed; Jason and his mother were asleep in her room. She stripped off her dress and stockings and went into the kitchen in her underwear. There was half a bottle of blush wine in the refrigerator, and she filled a water glass.

Randall had beautiful round crystal goblets. When she had broken one it really bothered him. "You don't understand; it's part of a set," he said, as if she were too ignorant to know a dozen matching wine glasses were a set. She went to Finlay's and bought a replacement for fifty-nine dollars she couldn't afford, and he took it as his due.

She wondered if he knew they were through. It had been brewing for months. He treated her like some sort of back-alley lay, wouldn't even let himself see how well they understood each other. It was a relief to have it settled, but she felt desolate. It hurt to break up, and it hurt to be grieving about someone who had given her so little.

They did have good times, when he wasn't afraid. It was true she'd been attracted to Randall by his money, by his ease. But as she got to know him, she quickly saw through his shell. Especially in bed after they made love, he would listen to her and talk to her, about all sorts of things. She could speak in the merest slanting reference, and he would understand. And sometimes he could be romantic. He had sent a card to her once at the office that said, *Thank you for a Glorious Fourth*. But she didn't see that side of him often enough. He was so concerned with his precious freedom, and she knew he was ashamed of her, thought she wasn't classy enough for him. It was always after their best times that he would freeze up, start criticizing her. But they were such a fine match in bed, where he could put aside all his pretensions and just play, sometimes for hours.

She carried her wine into the living room and sat in the comfortable chair. It was exhausting to think about what lay ahead. She knew just how it would be; she'd done it so many times before. First relief, then the numb, dumb grief, then endless crying, and thinking about everything that was wrong with her and Randall, then the soft sadness like a fog taking the shine off things, and then one day, after a few months, waking up free, feeling light and powerful with no one inhabiting her heart.

Nine

Randall had called an emergency Monday meeting of the Commission to consider the question of the sinkhole.

When Marybeth got the memo, she said to Luellen, her secretary, "What do you suppose we're going to consider? It's kind of like considering the moon, or a tornado."

She wasn't at all sure of Randall's authority to call an emergency meeting—he hadn't followed the proper procedure— but she wasn't going to challenge him. It galled Randall when she knew something he didn't. Despite what he thought, she wanted him to succeed as Mayor. She'd been Mayor for two years, and she'd really studied the rules. The morning he was sworn in as Mayor she went to his office and gave him her rules book with her congratulations, but he was stiff with her, and before she'd turned all the way around he had stuck it in the bottom drawer.

Marybeth's family had been in Opakulla since before the Civil War. At family reunions, held every three years, there were more than two hundred people, most of them named Coggins. When her father died, she took over Coggins Hardware and married her third cousin Munro, who worked there too.

All she'd ever really wanted to do was sell hardware. She didn't get involved in politics until her youngest was in high school. But she'd been wanting to put her two cents in ever since the fight over expanding the store. It seemed like the City Commission back then would open all the doors and lay down a red carpet too for the big companies from down south or out of state, but when it came to helping the little homegrown businesses, they wrapped them around with regulations and restrictions till they didn't have room to wiggle.

In the end they got the variance for Coggins Hardware, but she grew plenty of gray hairs in the process, and Munro lost most all of his. When the city and county decided to consolidate, and formed a seven-seat Commission, it was like musical chairs, with ten seats reduced to seven and all the city and county Commissioners marching in a circle with their bottoms stuck out ready to drop into a chair when the music stopped. Marybeth slipped in and got herself elected while they were all watching each other.

—•—

The other Commissioners had come in and taken their seats. It was a funny way to set up a meeting, she thought, with all of them lined up in a row. She had to lean over to look down the table and see whoever she was talking to.

Randall banged the gavel and began to speak, laying out the issue. Marybeth watched the sky putting on a show through the narrow windows. It was bright blue, with fluffy white clouds. She poured herself a glass of water and when she looked again, the white clouds were being chased away by towering thunderheads, turning darker and grayer by the minute. Then came the first flash, so close that she was still seeing its after-

64

image when the thunder came. It was early in the year for a storm like this. *Shining and thunder*—those damn words again. They were telling her something, but she didn't know what.

Would they ever get started?   Randall's introductory remarks were more like after-dinner speeches.

"We need to consider whether a special allocation will be necessary, and I've asked the manager to come here today to describe possible budget adjustments."

Cleve Bannister stood and went to the podium. He was a blonde, doughy man, who stayed pink and damp even in air conditioning.

Eight thousand dollars available from the fire department because of a rebate they'd received on their maintenance contract. Nine thousand five hundred from social services for a lapsed position. Twelve from the reserve funds. Without waiting for the Mayor to recognize her, Marybeth interrupted him.

"Now wait a minute. You want to spend thirty thousand dollars to do what?"

"Excuse me ma'am, but it's not thirty thousand dollars. It's twenty-nine thousand five hundred."

Randall spoke.

"We've already made it clear, I thought, that the precise approach has not yet been determined, but we want to be sure the money is available when we find out what can be done."

"Let me get this straight. You're planning to stop the sinkhole."

"We want to limit its growth, and when it has been stabilized, we're hoping we can begin to fill it in."

"Who have you been talking to, Randall? You might as well try to push those thunderheads across the sky before they rain on us. A sinkhole grows till it stops."

"Well, Commissioner Coggins, in my opinion it would be a shame to rely on folk wisdom about these things, when we can call on experts to help us. That's why I've asked Mr. Bannister to get in touch with the geology and engineering departments at the University. We hope to have one of the professors present some information at a future meeting."

Folk wisdom, dear God. Randall was another one of these Yankees come down to tell the simple folk of the South how to do things better. She couldn't believe she was still hearing that sort of thing from him; he'd been in Opakulla seven years.

"Well, if your experts can find a way to do it, I want you to know that I'll oppose spending tax dollars. Why don't you get Wilson Trust to pay for it? That's who you're doing it for anyway."

"We're doing it to preserve the Marsh, Commissioner, and I'm sure the Wilson Trust will be happy to contribute to our efforts."

"I gather you've already been talking to them. Sometimes, Randall, I wonder just who it is you think elected you."

"You're out of order, Commissioner."

She knew she was. But it made her so mad.

The meeting ended right at the height of the storm. It was only February, but it looked like they were finally going to have a wet spring again. Great gusts of wind blew pouring sheets of rain; it looked as though the whole sky were shifting. By the time she reached her car, even her underwear was soaked. It took almost half an hour to drive home, driving blind at fifteen miles an hour.

Munro was at the store. She had the house to herself. She hung her wet clothes in the laundry room and put on her pink quilted bathrobe. She carried a glass of iced tea into the living room, smiling. She could see herself sitting out on a porch, rocking, smoking a pipe, dispensing folk wisdom.

She settled down in a corner of the couch, staring out the picture window into the backyard. The sun was breaking through, lighting the long lines of rain, hypnotizing her, so she sat for almost a quarter of an hour with not a connected thought. She didn't stir until the rain ended. When the rain stops, the mockingbird sings. There he was, singing out from his fence post, while the water was still gushing from the downspout, splashing in a puddle. Her back garden, so beautifully tended, had been washed clean, the annuals battered, weighted down with water.

On the table beside the couch was a glass bowl filled with sharks' teeth. She spilled them out in her lap. They were like tiny Indian arrowheads, gleaming obsidian. She ran her fingernail along their serrated edges. In her junior year of high school, she and Billy Williams would go to the Marsh on Saturday afternoons, hunting shark's teeth. When they were worn out from pushing through the brush, and the heat of the sun, they'd go swimming in Cypress Lake. Billy would spread his blanket out on the ground, and they'd lie looking up at the sky darkening in the trees, watch the stars come out. Pretty soon Billy wasn't looking at the stars.

She'd seen Billy at the last reunion. He lived in Oklahoma now, with his wife and kids. How did he live on that empty yellow ground with nothing but oil wells growing? Of course, she'd never been there, wasn't even sure she'd ever seen pictures. But it couldn't be as nice as Opakulla. She'd have to go out to the Marsh with Munro, see what the lake looked like, all dried up.

Ten

It was past midnight, but Tyler was still in his office. The fluorescent lights were buzzing and his head ached. He had been at it since five o'clock, standing up and sitting down again, writing a line and deleting it, making notes and starting over. He'd tried to use his sinkhole lecture from Geology 101, but everything in it referred back to basic principles, and the Commission wouldn't know anything about geology. He'd taken his first draft to Gerald.

"You can't go in there talking about karst topography and piezometric surfaces, Waites. You have to talk to them in language they can understand. Make it into a story."

So here he was in the middle of the night in his tiny cluttered office. He might be the rising star of the geology department, but the geology department was nobody's rising star, cramped into old Mackenzie Hall, fighting for space with the four human fossils who had refused to move to the new museum with the rest of the archaeologists.

Tyler's office was in the basement. True, he had two windows, but they were right up by the ceiling. All he could see through them was the stair rail, and sometimes feet walking down. The previous occupant had painted the exposed pipes bright red, but otherwise everything was colorless and drab, steelcase desk littered with reports, metal shelves to the ceiling with rows and rows of manila folders. He ran a pencil along the nearest row, ruffling the flimsy papers poking out the ends, and stared into space.

—•—

Randall arrived early for the Commission meeting. He liked to sit in the center chair, his gavel in front of him, and savor the peace of the empty chamber. It was an afternoon peace, like the quiet, cool light of a museum. Slender beams of blonde oak curved up from the floor to meet in the center of the ceiling. Between the beams the deep-set windows looked like paintings: people crossing the plaza under the spreading live oak and bright blue sky. It was a brilliant use of nature to light and decorate without overwhelming. On the rear wall were photographs of former Commissioners. Someday his own portrait would hang there.

The chamber was filling up. Randall nodded at the regulars. Hilda Morse ran for office every two years and was rumored to be eyeing Marybeth's seat. Chance Jefferson wrote convoluted letters to the *Opakulla Chronicle* several times a year. He never used a single word where six would do. Randall couldn't understand why the *Chronicle* kept publishing them, until he learned that Chance's wife was the editor's cousin.

At the side of the chamber sat Paul, everything he owned clutched in his lap or strapped into the basket hanging from his wheelchair. Randall didn't bother to nod to him. Even awake, Paul didn't seem to be aware of anything beyond his little home on wheels. His lips were always moving, and sometimes when the mumble grew too loud one of the police officers who stood by the door would lean over and shush him. Yet he knew enough to be there promptly at two, every other Wednesday, rolling himself painfully down the street from under the bookstore awning where he spent his mornings.

Professor Waites hadn't arrived yet when the meeting began. He still hadn't appeared by the time Deputy Richard Selvedge, the third speaker, was winding up his report on the sheriff's new dispatching system. Randall was getting very anxious.

"Thank you, Deputy..." he had just started to say when Tyler, followed by Carol, came through the rear door of the chamber. The sight of Carol knocked the officer's name out of Randall's head. He repeated his thanks, this time with a period after it. What could she possibly be doing here? He knew that she was a secretary in the geology department. But she couldn't be here to take notes on Waites' speech. It was obvious, from the papers in his hand, that he had it all written out. Maybe she had come to see Randall. Of course. He was surprised by the warmth that flooded through him. She would watch him at his work, sitting at the center of the Commission, controlling the meeting like a conductor with his orchestra.

Randall called the next item on the agenda.

"And now we have Dr. Tyler Waites, who will be explaining our options with regard to the new sinkhole. We certainly appreciate your coming today, Dr. Waites. Is that microphone a little high? Joe, help him adjust it please."

After Tyler got the mic adjusted and had picked up the pages he'd knocked onto the floor, he began.

Elegantly, thought Randall, he described how the lake had disappeared: as if a plug had been pulled in a basin, and all the water had swirled away. He went on to tell of the sinking of the ground, and how this was just the latest in a continuous series of sinkholes that had shaped the Marsh basin itself. He explained collapse sinks and subsidence sinks. He told them of all the efforts that had been made to stop other sinkholes. He spoke for twenty minutes, then stood, rumpled and calm, waiting for questions.

Randall had enjoyed the presentation, although he hadn't paid close attention. He could pick up the gist of a report very quickly. He often said that he liked serving on the Commission because it forced him to become an instant expert in so many different areas.

Marybeth's light was on; she wanted to say something. Maybe she would apologize for her remarks at the previous meeting. Unlikely. He acknowledged her.

"Professor Waites, as I understand it, you're saying that all those attempts to stop other sinkholes were failures."

"That's right. You really can't stop a sinkhole in progress. You just have to wait. Then once it's finished collapsing, or eroding, you may be able to fill it in, though you have to be careful you don't contaminate the aquifer."

"How large is it now?"

"I haven't been out there since last Thursday, and at that time I measured it at a little over thirty meters."

"That's about thirty yards?"

"Approximately."

"And is there any way for you to tell how much longer it's going to go on growing?"

"No, there really isn't. I've seen new activity every time I've gone out there. The problem is that the whole area appears to be like a honeycomb under the surface. This isn't one sinkhole but many sinkholes. It may prove to be one of the most significant sinks we've seen."

Randall couldn't believe what he was hearing. He had to step in and stop this.

"Commissioner Coggins, perhaps you would allow other Commissioners an opportunity to speak?"

Waites had promised to come explain to the Commission the technology for controlling sinkholes. Randall started to speak but remembered what he had heard once about cross-examining witnesses—never ask a question you don't know the answer to. Why hadn't he listened more closely when he talked to Waites on the phone? What had he said? Yes, he would come tell the Commission about previous attempts to control sinkholes. The idiot. Why didn't he say that none of them had worked?

He looked down the room at Carol. She caught his eye and smiled at him. Did she understand that this professor had just made a fool of him? Was she feeling sorry for him? No, she couldn't know that Waites had disappointed him, if only Marybeth wouldn't say anything. Mercifully, she didn't.

"Thank you so much, Professor Waites, for agreeing to come here and share your knowledge with us. I know all the Commissioners will agree that your presentation was very interesting."

—•—

Tyler and Carol slipped out the back of the chamber. Tyler had driven his car to school that morning because he didn't want to risk being caught in the rain. On his way out the door to go to the meeting, Carol had stopped him to ask about it. She was obviously interested, so on an impulse he invited her to go along.

Now it was almost five o'clock.

"Do you need to go back to the office, or would you like me to drop you at your house?"

"My car's in the shop so I rode in with Judy. And Gerald's out of town. Might as well be hung for a sheep as a lamb."

She seemed to think Gerald kept track of her time, that he would care if she left work a little early. Obviously she didn't know Gerald very well. He drove north on Broward Avenue, toward her neighborhood. Nice old houses from the 1920s, city houses on tiny lots, with deep front porches and little backyards.

"Would you like to come in for some coffee?"

The front porch at Carol's was cluttered. They made their way around a tricycle, a baby swing, stacks of empty flowerpots, a bag of plant food slumped against the wall. Carol led him up the stairs, which ended awkwardly, with no landing, at the door to her apartment.

"I need to run downstairs and see what the kids are doing. My neighbor keeps them after school. I'll be right back."

Tyler sat in the big soft armchair under a bay window. In Carol's apartment he felt at home right away. The living room was full of shady afternoon light, filtered through the big magnolia in the front yard. African violets bloomed on a low shelf under the window. Through a wide arch he could see bright and goofy drawings on the refrigerator. The apartment seemed eager for the children to return, everything suspended there waiting for them, the Flashman comic face down on the couch, the grubby pink doll with her naked bottom so rudely in the air,

An only child, Tyler had spent four weeks every summer with his six cousins in Maryland, arriving always to their exuberant welcome. In Carol's apartment he felt the same invitation: if he was too shy to play, at least to look, to enjoy the clutter and noise.

He heard a soft step and then the door opened.

"Good news. The kids are watching a video downstairs and they don't want to come up yet. What can I get you?" She opened the refrigerator. "I have some beer."

But looking past her he could see there was just one, and he suggested coffee instead.

Tyler had never had very much to do with women. His parents had sent him to a boys' day school after they moved to Akron, where he quickly became engrossed in his science classes. In college he led a quiet and orderly life. Monastic, some would have called him, and although he had friends who were girls, he had no girlfriends.

Tyler had never intended to be celibate, but he found geology entirely absorbing. He woke each day with an eagerness to learn more about the earth. He loved to know the secrets buried under the streets and houses, under the smooth green lawns. He loved to dig and find the earth's oldest stories, from the time before storytellers. When night came, he lay down tired and satisfied, his mind filled with more amazing facts, slowly closing the gaps in his understanding, sometimes finding a new connection of his own in the floating time just before he slept.

In graduate school he had finally slept with a woman, a quiet, homely graduate assistant who worked on his research team. He found Wanda's body a pleasure and a comfort, but from the beginning their lovemaking was as simple and plain as bread. For two years they lived together like a long-married couple. Both were passionate about their work and contented with each other. Or so Tyler thought, until he came home from a field trip to find she had taken all her things and left a note: "Tyler, you have been very sweet. I can't deceive you anymore. I'm going to Chicago for a week with Vlad. I hope we can still be friends."

Vladimir Varonesky was an assistant professor in the political science department. He was dark, brooding, and rather stupid, Tyler thought.

The loss of Wanda was a blow, but she had taken up such a small part of his attention that it wasn't long before he was comfortable again in his solitude. He had no further romantic adventures. This bothered his mother. She felt that once established in his career he should be searching for a wife. "There's no reason you can't find someone, Tyler, you're a nice-looking man." Even his mother wouldn't think to call him handsome. His light brown hair was thinning on top. His eyes looked a bit washed-out, pink and rabbit-y behind his glasses. He had been lean, almost scrawny, until well into his twenties, but by thirty he had finally filled out, and some of the too-sharp angles in his face had softened.

He did have brief seasons of loneliness. They came on him suddenly, inexplicably. He would wake up one morning to a different stillness in his apartment, an emptiness. Then for days the streets were filled with couples, women in grocery stores pushed loaded carts, men rode by on bicycles towing babies behind them. If he went to the Marsh for refuge, its magic failed him. The crunch of leaves beneath his feet, light flowing through the treetops and shimmering on the water, the green and flowery smells, the rustle and birdsong, couldn't reach him. He stayed closed tight inside himself, his senses all shut down. Then, as suddenly as it had come, the loneliness would vanish. He would wake to a room no longer empty, but filled with peace.

Tyler couldn't imagine searching for a wife. A wife would come to him as everything else had. Time would pass, and he would continue on the same path, and one day she would join him. This didn't stop him from examining each woman he encountered to see if she might be the one. He had long since examined Carol and rejected her. She was kind and warm, but she was too sleek, her appearance too perfect, her hair and makeup always just so. She scared him just a little. He preferred a healthy, natural look.

Now all her careful polish was gone. How did she come from this warm, lively place to sit at the front desk every day, cool and distant, patient and calm? Always a sympathetic word as a professor grumbled about exams to grade or a late travel reimbursement, as Gerald stood behind her fussing about the memo he wanted by noon. It seemed as if the department were her only and all-important life, as if the tiny formal photo of the children in a cheap frame on the corner of her desk were nothing but decoration. Now he realized she put that woman on every morning with her makeup, like a costume. This woman, looking larger and a little disheveled now that she had shed her jacket, sitting back in the wicker settee with her stockinged feet on the coffee table, was the real Carol. How many of the other people he saw every day had these full lives around them, while he went home every night to his quiet apartment?

Carol rubbed her feet. The coffee finished brewing. She looked so comfortable, so tired.

"You sit there. I'll get it," he said.

When he came back in with a cup for each of them, she had a funny look on her face.

"You know, you're a very nice man."

It almost sounded like a decision.

"I thought your speech was really interesting. I've never heard you teach before. You made it sound like a story."

"Actually, Gerald helped me a lot with it. I'm not sure he was satisfied with it, though. He told me I was being too pessimistic."

"What did you think of Randall?"

"Who?"

"Commissioner Fairchild."

"I didn't form much of an impression, really. I was kind of nervous. He seems to know what he's doing. But I'm not sure he was listening to me. When that other Commissioner, the woman, finished with her questions I got the feeling he was surprised. Actually, he seemed angry."

"I used to go out with him. We just broke up a month ago."

"Oh, well, I didn't mean anything. I think he's quite impressive."

"That's okay, you can't offend me. And you could never be as impressed by Randall as he is by himself."

Tyler was uncomfortable. He was afraid she was going to start talking about her affair with Randall. He was sure it had been an affair, something about the way she had said it, the casual contempt with a trace of anger.

"Have you been out to see the sinkhole?"

"No. My grandfather used to take me sliding at the Punchbowl. I take the kids now—you can't slide there anymore, but they think the stairs are fun. Is the new one anything like that?"

"I think it's bigger. And it's nothing but rubble—it's what the Punchbowl would have looked like a thousand years ago. It's fascinating to see it just beginning. How old are your children? They might enjoy it."

"Robin is eight, and Christopher is almost six."

"Do they like hiking?"

She laughed.

"I wouldn't call what they do hiking. Have you ever gone for a walk with children?"

"I guess I never have. Not since I was one myself."

"It's kind of a slow process. And if you're talking about any kind of distance, lots of whining. Maybe we ought to take them somewhere less rugged, a picnic in the park or something. Then you could get an idea yourself of what they're fit for."

Was she asking him out? Or had he asked her out?

"Maybe this Saturday we could take them to the botanical gardens," he said.

"That would be nice. They like the meadow. I could fix a picnic."

He was suddenly anxious to leave before the children came upstairs.

—•—

Vernell was talking to the bacon sizzling on the grill as Tyler walked in the next morning.

"That man is all mouth and no ears."

She turned around as the door banged behind him.

"Who are you talking about, Vernell?"

"The Reverend Dr. Taylor Malcolm Hughes, just been at the church three months, wants to tell me how to run the Spring Flowers Dinner."

She rolled an onion to the middle of the chopping block and sliced fiercely, her thick forearm pumping up and down like a piston.

"I saw you in the paper this morning." Jared had eased the screen door closed and walked in so quietly Tyler didn't know he'd come in until he spoke.

Vernell turned around and glared at Tyler. "What are you doing in the paper?"

"I spoke to the Commission yesterday about the new sinkhole that's forming out in the Marsh."

"That's the biggest one we've ever had, isn't it?" Jared asked.

"It's not quite as big as the Punchbowl, but it hasn't stopped sinking, and it may yet be."

"Remember how we used to go sliding in the Punchbowl before they turned it into a park? Did you ever go there as a child, Vernell?"

"With all them white boys cutting the fool out there?"

She went on slicing the onions. She still hadn't brought Tyler any coffee, and he could tell she was going to chop up every one of those onions before she started on his breakfast.

"No, Jared, you wouldn't catch me out there. And if my mama did, she'd of let me know about it. No little black girl with a lick of sense would have gone anywhere near it."

She broke the awkward silence that followed.

"What's this new one look like, Tyler?"

"Rubble, nothing but rubble. Like a lunatic went in with a huge steam shovel."

"So what did the Commissioners want to know?"

"Well, it was strange. Apparently, Commissioner Fairchild thought I was going to be able to advise them how to stop it from getting any bigger, maybe tell them how to fill it in."

Here came Vernell's rare laugh. Tyler loved to hear it.

"If they want to start filling in holes we got some potholes over to Miller's End could use some work."

"Vernell, I really don't know if Commissioner Fairchild was listening to me."

"Politicians and preachers, they're all the same. Big mouth, no ears."

Eleven

After the meeting, Randall headed for the back stairs. He didn't want to have to talk to anybody. If he'd been paying attention, he would have seen where Professor Waites' report was leading, and he probably could have cut it short. But Carol had distracted him. Watching her, he could feel her warm face pressed against his shoulder, smell her hair. She had made him look like a fool. It must have been obvious to everybody that Dr. Waites had taken him by surprise. The lobby was clear, but as he headed toward the exit, he heard the unmistakable drawl of Norris Freel.

"Oh, Commissioner."

He'd been lurking against the wall, where the door concealed him as it opened. Norris was the closest thing to an investigative reporter the *Chronicle* had. He might be a sloppy writer, and a little dense, but he had mastered persistence. Well, there was no escaping it. And maybe there was some way to slant things so Randall could save face in the paper.

"What's your reaction to Professor Waites' report?"

"He provided us some valuable information. We will be conferring with other faculty from the university as to how we can proceed with this."

"It sounds as if there really isn't any way to proceed."

After all, Norris was only a little dense.

"That was just one man's opinion. Professor Waites is undoubtedly an expert on sinkholes, but he doesn't know anything about engineering. It's marvelous what can be accomplished nowadays."

"Does the county have enough money to repair the damage?"

"I can't say at this point. We will have to wait until we have the experts' recommendations. I have found almost thirty thousand dollars from various sources, as I reported at our last meeting. And we can always draw more from the contingency fund."

"Do you think the other Commissioners will go along with that? Seems like Commissioner Coggins, at least, would oppose it."

"Commissioner Coggins is entitled to her opinion, of course. But we certainly cannot allow the lakeside landowners to lose the value of their property. As citizens and taxpayers, they are entitled to county services like anyone else. Now, if you'll excuse me please."

The report was definitely disturbing, and Randall could only hope he had succeeded in fooling Norris. Everything else aside, what on earth would he do about his deposit on Sunrise Terrace? The lake gone, the land crumbling. Waites had said it was growing away from the Trust land, but still, would it be safe to live so near a sinkhole? Suppose he did go ahead and buy there, and then everything caved in. He'd be buying nothing but a lawsuit. Waites might be only a professor at a third-rate university, but Randall knew that he was a leader in his field. And he probably didn't need to know anything about engineering to know that a sinkhole couldn't be stopped.

—•—

Randall was surprised to find he was hungry when he got home. He took half an acorn squash and some chicken out of the refrigerator. He liked to cook. He liked the feel of food, the smells, liked the way the tasks of cooking occupied half his mind, leaving the other half free to wander. Clearly, Carol hadn't come to the meeting to see him. She'd left as soon as Waites finished with his talk. But maybe she had come to see him and then changed her mind. Maybe she was a little intimidated, watching him preside over the meeting. Should he call her? He could make it casual, of course. Wouldn't want her to think he was interested in getting back together.

He had called her once after the scene in his apartment. She had sounded subdued, tired. She hadn't been cruel, but she was implacable, and had refused to see him. "Randall, I really mean it. You and I just aren't going to work out." It made him rather angry, after all the times she'd nagged him to talk about their relationship. After he hung up, his face burning, he swore he wouldn't call her again. But seeing her sitting there shook his resolve.

He filled the squash with chopped garlic, pine nuts, and plenty of butter, and put it in the microwave while the chicken broiled. He had greens for a salad, but no bread. He should have stopped at the French bakery on the way home. Those rare weekends when Carol could spend the night, they used to drive to the bakery in the morning to get croissants. He always sent her in to get them. As long as he'd studied French in college, he was never comfortable with his pronunciation. She'd come back and jump in the car. "Here's your crescent rolls, Rrrandy," with a passable French "r." He hated being called Randy, and she knew it.

Sometimes he felt that she understood him too well. But it was wonderful, whatever they talked about, she always knew what he was getting at. She wasn't stupid by any means, merely uneducated. Early in their relationship he had encouraged her to read, but then he would find the books he gave her lying face down, open in the middle of the first chapter. "I'm too tired at night to read all that heavy stuff," she told him. "Once the kids are in bed, all I want to do is watch TV, or maybe read a magazine."

She was a good mother, he had to give her that, although she focused too much on the children. A little benign neglect was good for children, though he knew better than to raise the topic with her. And it would be nice if she could keep them better groomed. They always seemed to have holes in the knees of their pants. It wasn't a question of money. When they had something nice they didn't take care of it. He had bought Robin an expensive plaid wool jacket for her birthday the year before and the next time he saw it the shoulder was torn.

When he had finished dinner, he put the dishes in the sink and went into the living room. He was surrounded by music all day at the radio station but he couldn't really listen; there was too much work to do. He looked forward to a free evening.

Others preferred the concert hall, but Randall didn't like listening to music in public. In public he always had to close his eyes. He knew it seemed affected, but he couldn't bear to see others seeing him naked. He closed his eyes when he was making love too, though he loved to watch a woman's face, and catch glimpses of her body. But the moment she opened her eyes, he would close his.

The sound was better too, at home. No rustling, no coughing, no architect's acoustics that thinned out the treble and swallowed up the bass. His music systems, digital and analog, had cost more than his car. The components were stark, sleek black, with naked speakers and visible bolts that gave them the look of laboratory equipment. From the shelf above the receiver a head of Buddha, impaled on a spiked pedestal, gazed benevolently down at him in his leather lounge chair.

He relaxed, waiting for the joy, the tenderness of Martinu's Fourth to carry him off. But instead, there was Carol again. Or rather, there wasn't Carol. It was a surprise when she told him they were through. It was a bigger surprise that she had left such a hole in his life. It didn't make sense. He hadn't seen her more than once a week. She seldom came to his place. But now, without her curled on the couch, he couldn't relax in his chair. The image of the other night, of Carol as a permanent fixture, kept coming back to haunt him. She was more present now than she had been when they were together.

If he called her, what would he say? *I saw you at the Commission meeting.* So what? He could pretend he was calling to discuss the professor's testimony. But she'd see through him. She always did. When he told her about his interview with Adrienne Shelby, she knew right away that they'd slept together. She didn't make much of a fuss, just said his brains were in his balls, crude as usual, and she hoped he'd used a condom. She'd insisted they use condoms since she first realized he was likely to sleep with other women. "I had all the jealousy burned out of me by the first man I fell in love with. And I'm not in love with you, so I don't give a damn what you do," she'd said. He couldn't tell whether she was lying.

In their happy times, after making love, she talked as if she did love him. It was then that he was most uncomfortable. She would question him: have you ever been as happy with anybody else? What's your favorite thing about me? They always felt like trick questions. She was storing the answers away, waiting to catch him in inconsistencies. He never could understand women. They'd be attracted to a man and then start peeling his personality away layer by layer. What if it were all layers, like an onion?

He longed for intimacy as much as the next man, and he thought he would have liked to be open with her. It was all his mother's fault. Even when he was little, she used to ask him how he felt about everything, and if he didn't answer, she'd describe his feelings for him. It made him shudder to think of it. And every morning he and his two brothers were supposed to report their dreams. When they couldn't remember, they would make them up, but she always knew. The stories were too orderly, or too relentlessly exciting. "It's important to remember your dreams, my dears. It's how we tidy up before the day begins." Randall was twelve when Bennett, fourteen, looked their mother straight in the face and described a wet dream. Tears rose in her eyes. She excused him from the table, though he hadn't touched his cereal, and she never asked about their dreams again.

They'd already reached the Largo, and he hadn't heard a note. He just didn't have it in him tonight to concentrate. Now that he was ready to talk to Carol, she refused. She'd ruined the Commission meeting. She was ruining his music. He'd be damned if he'd call her. He stood up and went to the cabinet, looking for something more appropriate to his state of mind. He put on the Borodin string quartet playing Shostakovich and sat down again in his chair. He hadn't bothered to turn on the lights, and the sky through the window was already deeper than dusk. He sat in the gloom, the mournful adagios washing through him, and watched the lurid green lights on the equalizer flickering up and down.

Twelve

The children were playing outside, and Carol was in the kitchen stripping meat off a turkey carcass. Peanut butter for the kids' sandwiches, but turkey salad for her and Tyler, and she'd bought some nuts to dress it up. Though Tyler seemed like he wouldn't notice what he was eating.

He didn't notice what he wore. He came into work every day in the same khaki pants. They couldn't actually be the same because they were always clean, if rumpled, but he must buy them all at once, probably at Stop and Save. And plaid shirts, flannel in winter, short-sleeved cotton the rest of the year. What did Randall spend on his clothes? His dry-cleaning bill alone would probably buy all of Tyler's clothes, and hers too.

Tyler, what was it about Tyler? He felt like a friend, not a lover. There was something pudgy-looking about him, though he wasn't fat. It was more the shape of his face: soft chin, round cheeks, round nose. He wasn't good-looking, but he looked nice. Even through the thick glasses you could see his smiling eyes.

He wasn't sexy, but she was tired of sex, though her body said no, her body was getting restless. Randall was so smooth, so silky, she still could feel every inch of him, his surprising bulk when she stretched her arms around him, crisp curly hair between her fingers, the soft skin of his side, his big tight balls banging against her. She was horny, but tired of everything that went with sex, all the hope and speculation, reaching out and being disappointed. Let someone into your life, or more like it, try and shape your life around theirs. Get the kids to disappear. Sneak out of the bedroom early to fix their breakfast, and sneak back in for another hour, lock the bedroom door. Pay a babysitter and put off the light bill. Hiding your own world, always on trial in his.

She felt comfortable with Tyler. He was comfortable with himself. But he had said he was nervous giving his talk to the Commission. He'd even dropped his papers. Randall would never admit to being nervous. He sat up there in charge of the whole Commission, cock of the walk. Even when he saw her and lost his place, he covered it up so only she could tell. That was the kind of man who attracted her, the kind who seemed confident and powerful. Even knowing him as she did, anxious and fussy with a fragile little ego, she wanted to attach herself to that smooth shell. She liked walking into a party, knowing that everyone knew she was with him, and everyone knew who he was. Now she'd seen him in his power, and it looked a little silly. Did the mayor of Atlanta sit around listening to people drone on about dispatchers and drainage? Good thing she had never gone to a Commission meeting when they were still together.

She was half dressed before it occurred to her that this was a date, her first since she'd broken up with Randall. But it didn't feel like a date, with children in tow, with Tyler that she saw every day. It was like going out with her brother. She changed from her old jeans to new ones and tried on three tops before settling on one that was pretty, but not sexy.

Gloomily she stood at the counter slicing carrots. Here she was, making a meal for a man again when she ought to be avoiding them entirely. If he wanted to see her so much why couldn't he take her out someplace nice? She'd spent all her spare change on almonds. But when the bell rang and she opened the door, there he stood, smiling, eyelids pink behind those ugly glasses with transparent frames. Why be angry at him? Really, she had maneuvered him into asking her out. He looked uncomfortable standing there. She invited him in.

"Can I help?"

"You can chop these nuts. I'm sorry I'm late getting this ready."

"Oh, that's all right. I think I'm a little early."

The children came in, and Christopher, of course, went straight to Tyler.

"Are you coming on our picnic? I'm going to sit in the front seat with you."

At least he hadn't asked if Tyler was going to be their new daddy, as he had asked the man who was fixing the stove last month.

When it came time to get in the car, she put Christopher firmly in the back, raising her eyebrows at him as she saw a whine about to escape.

"Do you want to have fun on this picnic, Christopher?"

"Yes, ma'am."

At the gardens, they parked and walked down the azalea trail to the meadow, which rose gently from the shore of Palm Lake. They started with a game of kicking the soccer ball around. Robin and Christopher were up on the slope and Carol and Tyler down on the shore, desperately trying to stop the ball from rolling into the water as the kids kicked it with more ferocity than skill. When they were thoroughly breathless and sweaty, they spread out Tyler's old blanket at the top of the meadow, under a tree. Even in early March it was almost hot enough for swimming, but Palm Lake was full of alligators.

Christopher held Tyler's binoculars, staring intently out at the little island in the middle of the lake, where two alligators lay sprawled in the sun. To the naked eye they were nothing more than small black curves, like scraps of blown tires.

"Hey, neat," said Christopher.

"Let me see," said Robin.

"No, I gotta watch this."

"What are they doing?"

"I gotta watch this guy. I'll tell you later."

The alligators weren't moving at all.

"Wow," murmured Christopher, just loud enough for Robin to hear.

"Mommy, he won't let me have a turn."

"Christopher, it's Robin's turn," Carol said automatically. She was lying on the blanket, staring up into the clouds. She paid no more attention to the kids than to the inchworm that was crawling in her hair. Tyler reached over and lifted it off.

Robin had the binoculars now, focusing on an egret.

"Hey, man! The gators are moving; look over there!"

"I'm watching this bird, Christopher. When it's your turn again you can look at the alligators if you want."

"Mom, there's one gator crawling on top of the other and she won't even look. It's my turn anyway."

Carol sighed and sat up.

"If you two can't take turns, Tyler will put the binoculars in the car. I think it's time for lunch."

She'd packed sandwiches and carrots, fruit and cookies. Tyler was embarrassed at the stinginess of his offering, a big bag of potato chips and a six pack of Coke.

"Oh wow, Mom never lets us have Coke. But we have to drink it or we'll be too thirsty, right Mom?"

"Right, Christopher. Especially if you don't stop eating all those potato chips."

"Sorry, I guess I wasn't thinking," Tyler said.

"Oh, that's okay, I don't buy it for them, but there's nothing wrong with it once in a while. Move the chips away from me though. I could eat them all myself."

"Here, I'll trade you the carrots."

For a few minutes even Robin was silent.

"It's so peaceful here," Carol sighed.

She had finished most of her sandwich, and was lying on her stomach, propped on her elbows, eating an apple. Tyler realized that to her, it probably did feel peaceful, though he was surprised their clamor hadn't chased away the egret. With the kids busy eating, he could hear the insects again.

The air was cool and the sun hot on his bare arms. A wood thrush had found a perch high in one of the old azaleas and was singing fiercely at two cardinals who were courting in the lower branches.

Suddenly Christopher screamed, a throat-grating, ear-piercing scream. Carol froze for a moment, and then dropped the apple and lunged for him with her arms open.

"He got bit by a bee, he got bit by a bee!" yelled Robin.

And Tyler saw, in the lump of chewed sandwich that had fallen out of Christopher's mouth when he screamed, the crushed body of a yellow jacket. Carol was all calm action, issuing instructions.

"Robin, go get the toys. Tyler, will you pack things up? We need to get him to the hospital."

And all the while Christopher went on screaming.

"Christopher darling, hush now, hush now," and she knelt and held him tight against her, rocking back and forth.

The speed limit on the park road was fifteen miles an hour. Christopher was silent now, and very quietly Carol said, "Can you go faster? He's having trouble breathing."

Tyler sped up.

At the hospital Carol carried Christopher to the door and backed through it, walked past the line of people and laid him on the counter.

"He's choking. He got stung in the tongue by a yellow jacket, and he's allergic."

Tyler stood watching with Robin. An orderly lifted Christopher onto a gurney while a nurse filled a hypodermic. In just a couple of minutes he was breathing more easily. Carol seemed to wilt as the hospital took over.

She looked around and saw Robin standing next to Tyler and said to her, with her voice shaking, "He's going to be okay honey, you don't have to be frightened."

The orderly was pushing the gurney toward the double doors beyond the counter, and Carol started to follow. Tyler stood off to the side, not sure what he should do.

"Look out for Robin, will you? Honey, you stay with Tyler, Christopher's going to be okay."

"Ma'am, you need to give us some information," the clerk said.

"Send the paperwork in here. I'm staying with my son."

She disappeared through the double doors, trailing behind the gurney.

Tyler turned to Robin. "Should we sit down over there?"

"I got stung by a bee once, here on my arm."

"Did you?"

"Did you ever get stung?"

"Yes I did, by a yellow jacket, just like your brother."

"You mean in the tongue?" Her eyes were wide again.

"No, not in the tongue. On my finger. It was at a picnic too, and I was reaching for a sandwich. Yellow jackets always come around picnics."

"Like ants. I did a report for my teacher on ants and I got an A."

"That's a good grade."

"It's the best grade. You can't have a better grade than an A unless you get an A plus and Mrs. Gustafson doesn't give A plusses."

Tyler wondered when Carol would be back.

"There's a store here in the hospital where they have candy and stuff."

"Would you like to go there?"

"Yes, we could buy candy for Christopher."

"And maybe for you?"

"OK, if you want to."

"What if your mom comes back and we're not here?"

"Oh, she won't be back for a long, long, long time. It takes a long time when you go to the emergency room."

"Well, I'll just tell this clerk where we're going so Carol won't be worried if she comes back."

But the clerk was talking to an old man who held his arm up, his hand wrapped in a bloody towel, and there were three other people waiting, so Tyler decided to risk it. Though he didn't have Robin's experience with emergency rooms, he knew they took a long time.

Through long tunnels of hallways, with humming fluorescent lights, they followed the color-coded signs to the lobby. In the store, Robin focused on the bins of nickel candy down near the floor, underneath the candy bars.

"Can I get four pieces for me and four for Christopher?"

"I guess so."

"What about five pieces?"

"No, why don't you just get four."

It took her almost ten minutes to choose, picking them up and considering them, putting them back. He thought someone would complain, but no one was paying any attention. Finally, she settled on two green and two pink for each of them. On an impulse, he bought a rose in a small plastic tube for Carol.

Carol and Christopher returned to the waiting room within minutes of Tyler and Robin. Christopher had apparently suffered no lasting damage, and his tongue was working fine. He proceeded to tell Robin everything they had done to him.

"I got them some candy; I hope you don't mind. And here, I got this for you."

"Why, thank you." Suddenly her face crumpled and she covered it with her hands. When she looked up again, her eyes were wet.

"Sorry. I'm afraid this hasn't been much of a picnic. Why don't we go back to my place and have some coffee."

—•—

Christopher, who had been frenetic in the car, fell asleep within five minutes of arriving home. Carol carried him into the children's room. Robin suggested they all play Old Maid, but Carol said, "No darling, I don't want to do anything right now but just sit."

Robin whined a little, but then disappeared into the bedroom. Carol started the coffee. She put the rose in a crystal bud vase, a Christmas present from Randall, who had never supplied the rose to fill it. She put the vase in the window, where it sent patches of rainbow onto the floor, and settled back in the corner of the sofa.

Tyler sat in the wicker chair opposite and watched her. She made no effort to speak. Her breathing was as slow and even as if she were sleeping. He thought that he should probably leave, but he found he wanted to be here with her. Quietly he got up and poured himself a cup of coffee, and then sat back down.

Despite everything, or was it because of everything, he had that same sense of ease that he had felt on his first visit. Carol with her complicated life was like a weaver, never hesitating, picking up even the jarring colors and blending them in. She had been so single-minded, so intense, from the moment Christopher screamed to the time they left the hospital and got back in the car, when she had slumped for a moment and let everything go slack. He felt how irrelevant he was to this world of hers, and that made him long to be a part of it, to be one of the yarns she picked up and attached to her shuttle, worked so smoothly into the cloth. He wanted to slip in and join this family she had already made.

Now she was asleep, and he thought there was no harm in sitting a few moments more, watching her. There were lines in her face that surely hadn't been there before. The flesh sagged a little, looking soft and downy. He would just finish his coffee and go. He stood up and she didn't stir. He had to kiss the soft skin there on her cheek.

As he did, she reached out and gave him a friendly pat on the hand, murmured, "Thanks for the rose. I'm glad you were here."

But she didn't try to stop him from leaving.

Thirteen

Jade and Jasmine were identical twins whose mother had shut her eyes to the big babies with carrot-colored fuzz on their heads and named them out of some tipsy notion of feminine beauty. They stayed hefty and red-headed. By the time they reached their teens, they were 5'10".

As children, they played like sisters and fought like sisters. Their mother never got crazy drunk; she just sipped all day, "to keep the edge off,' she told them brightly, when they were far too young to understand. When they were seven their father left, married again, and moved to Hawaii. By the time they were ten, Jade and Jasmine were pretty much on their own, and raising each other.

They had a gang of friends, but everyone knew that Jade never went anywhere without Jasmine, and Jasmine never went anywhere without Jade. They were best friends, and the other girls accepted that.

The twins started their periods within a month of each other, shortly after their eleventh birthday. At Melissa's twelfth birthday party only about half the group had hit puberty, but all of them were interested, or pretended to be, in boys.

"You were slow-dancing with Michael after the play," Melissa said to Jennifer.

"I was not."

"Everybody saw you. Do you know what that feels like? I'll show you. Jasmine, come over here and press up against Jennifer's back."

Jasmine complied. You always complied with Melissa.

"Eeew, that's gross," Jennifer said.

"Well that's what a boy feels when you slow-dance."

So then they all had to try it. Some of the girls, including Jennifer and the twins, but not including Melissa, had already developed substantial breasts. Melissa lined them up in pairs, and the breasted embraced the flat from behind.

"They're so big and squishy."

"Mine aren't."

"Let's look."

When they took off their shirts and bras they saw a variety of sizes and shapes they had never imagined.

"Oooh, yours look so firm. Mine are all floppy."

"That's just cause they're big. You're lucky; guys like big boobs."

"But mine are brown. I wish I had pink nipples like you."

They pranced and danced in front of the mirror. Jennifer showed them the pencil test – you put a pencil under your breast and if it stayed, they were too saggy.

Jasmine and Jade both flunked.

"There's an exercise you can do."

They stood in a circle, pulling on their elbows to engage their pecs, chanting, "I must, I must, I must increase my bust."

"But I don't want to get bigger," Nicole said.

"Well, this article said it makes them firm."

Melissa's mother knocked on the door.

"Don't come in! We're changing," Melissa called.

"I just wondered what you girls are up to. Do you want some popcorn? Or some more cake?"

"Sure. We're putting on our pajamas, and then we'll be down."

After cake, after watching *Porky's* and *Risky Business* on the VCR with popcorn, chips, and onion dip, they practiced kissing – little pecking kisses, long open-mouthed kisses, and everything they could imagine in between. Jasmine discovered how good it felt to kiss a girl, especially Nicole.

When they got home late the next morning, and were finally alone, they talked it all over.

"Do you think you're a lesbian?"

"I don't know, Jade. I just really liked it, and I thought about Nicole all night."

"Oooh, I better watch out around you."

"Don't be stupid, you're my sister."

"Yeah, and I think I like boys. The kissing was okay, but I'd like to try it with Rodney."

Jade didn't ever get to try it with Rodney, but by ninth grade she had tried kissing and plenty more with several boys. A lot of boys wanted to double date with the twins. A couple of times they agreed and spent the evening necking in the car with their dates. But it didn't do anything for Jasmine. She had a big crush on Nicole but was afraid to tell her. She listened avidly to Jade's stories of dealing with boys, but mostly avoided them. She just nurtured her fantasy love.

And then one day in junior year, by accident, she found out how Nicole felt. The twins never wore matching outfits, but they freely shared clothes. Sometimes they would switch identities for a day or two, to deal with the boredom of school, or to get back at a teacher they didn't like. Jasmine French-braided Jade's hair, and Jade ironed Jasmine's frizzy mop until it was smooth and sleek and fell past her shoulders. Carefully, she covered Jasmine's freckles with make-up and applied eyeliner and shadow. Her own face felt kind of naked with nothing on it, and her lips were dry without lipstick. But the disguise worked. When they stood together in front of the mirror, they confused themselves. It was oddly disorienting.

On one of those switch days, Nicole came over to Jasmine-as-Jade in the cafeteria. The twins had different lunch periods, and Jade and Nicole almost always ate together.

"Jade, do you think Jasmine likes me?"

"Sure she does. Why?"

"It's like she never wants to sit next to me. And one time, I touched her hand to tell her something, and she got pissed off."

"Oh, Jasmine can be kind of weird sometimes."

Jasmine remembered that time, as she remembered every time Nicole had spoken to her. She wanted so much to just come right out and tell her. To her astonishment, Nicole spoke first.

"Jade, can I tell you something and you swear you'll never tell?"

"Sure."

"It's just…I think I like girls."

"You mean, *like* them, like instead of boys?"

"Yeah."

"Oh my God."

"What? It's not that bad. You promised you wouldn't tell anyone, not even Jasmine."

"No, but…but…me too. I mean me, Jasmine. Oh God, Nicole, I'm not Jade, I'm Jasmine; sometimes we switch. And I don't like boys either. I like girls. I like you."

Their love affair lasted through senior year, and only Jade knew about it.

"You're lucky, Jas, being with Nicole. Sometimes I wish I liked girls. Boys can be so dense."

The guidance counselor urged the twins to go to different colleges. She knew about their switch days.

"You need individuation," she told them, and they agreed. At a little private college in Colorado, Jade joined the glee club, sat in at the Dean's office protest, ran cross country, and screwed everyone in pants, and a few in skirts, looking for something that mattered to her more than Jasmine. In Ohio, Jasmine was more focused. She joined an all-girl band and took up drums and the bass player.

—•—

In April of their sophomore year, two weeks before they were due home for the summer and right in the middle of finals, Jasmine called Jade.

"There's no point to this, Jade."

That she didn't need to explain was proof, if she needed any, that she was right.

"So what do you want to do?"

"If you want to finish school, I could move out there and get a job."

"Why should I finish school? How much money do you have?"

"About $900."

"Let's finish our exams, and then do some travelling."

Fourteen

The twins floated around the country for a couple of years, hitchhiking. They camped out or crashed with people they met on the road. When they needed money, they would work for a while – art modeling paid best, and they often found temporary lovers in the art classes and studios.

Once they visited their mother, who welcomed them, invited the relatives for a barbecue, and urged them to stay around a while.

"I wish I'd done what you're doing. You're so brave. I was too young when I married your father."

Jade didn't want to hear about their parents' marriage even one more time

"We're grown now, Jasmine. We don't need a mother. Let's leave her to her gin."

They never made it to Hawaii to see their father.

They were in Ann Arbor, wandering with the crowd through an arts fair, when they met Alan Carmody, who told them about his cousin Mark and Harmony Farm, off Route 19 in western Pennsylvania. They put up a notice on the rides board at the student union and found someone who was headed to Philadelphia.

Their ride dropped them off just past Buttonwood and gave them directions to the farm, so they arrived on foot. They stood in front of the gate, looking at the swinging sign. It was a rainbow with a treble clef at one end and bright red chords painted on the bands of color. The name Harmony Farm curved above the rainbow.

The house was some distance from the road, but they could hear the music. They saw two people beyond the house, lying on a blanket, barely visible in the high weeds.

"Jasmine. You see those two? I think they're naked."

Jasmine squinted and peered.

"I think you're right. Do you suppose we should get undressed?"

"No. I can't carry another thing, and besides, I'm not sure I can knock on a stranger's door with absolutely nothing on. We can always take off our clothes after they let us in."

"Oh, I hope they do let us in."

Jasmine realized later that she needn't have worried. They were two beautiful women, and they had all their savings in cash. Mark came to the door when they knocked. He was a tall, muscular man, with a great bush of graying hair pulled into a ponytail. He wasn't entirely naked: he wore a multi-colored crocheted cap. Behind him they saw two men in jeans, and a woman fully dressed, but with her blouse unbuttoned to nurse her baby.

Within a week the twins felt completely at home, part of the family. Separately and together they'd slept with every member of the commune, not excluding Lillian, the woman with the baby, whose milk dappled her nipples like dew as they caressed her breasts.

Mark had inherited the farm, which had been in the Carmody family for seven generations. It was 1975; he was playing drums with a bar band in New Jersey when his parents were killed. Early one morning in September, with mist rising from the fields and spilling over onto the road, they were driving to town to do the monthly shopping when a rock-truck driver rolled past a stop sign. They were killed instantly and buried on the spot under a truckload of pink granite. Mark came home, buried them properly, and stayed on in the farmhouse.

Neighbors helped him with the first harvest, and then, without any help, he planted a fine crop of marijuana behind the barn. Within six weeks he had eleven roommates, and milk production on the neighboring dairy farm increased dramatically as the cows became accustomed to Jefferson Starship.

As a boy, Mark had reluctantly absorbed considerable knowledge of farming, and with eleven willing workers it was easy to maintain a steady yield of the best marijuana in Pennsylvania. They developed their market by word of mouth. Mark had considered starting a mail order business, but the others convinced him that it wasn't worth the risk. Their needs were simple and dope was free. They were bringing in as much money as they wanted, and there was plenty of time for making love and music.

—•—

Jade and Jasmine stayed in the warm fog of sex and grass for over a year. A few people left, a few more came. New faces, new bodies blended into old. Each day was like the next. It was Jade who first began to feel restless. They were sitting behind the barn, playing with the new kittens.

"There's got to be something to do."

"But there's nothing to do, Mommy," whined Jasmine.

"Oh God, you remember what Mom used to say when we said that?"

"Get the List."

It was a list of chores that their mother kept in the kitchen, stuck between two cookbooks. Weed garden, polish silver, scrub charcoal grill, or the worst: clean venetian blinds. They hated the list, but several times each summer, one of them would forget and complain about having nothing to do. Useless for the other to protest that she was busy. "Don't you think you ought to help your sister?"

"Jas, why don't we make our own list? There's really a lot that needs doing around here. The place is falling apart. Someday one of us is going to break an ankle in that hole in the bathroom floor."

"Oh, all right. But you have to promise that you won't get all bossy on me. We only work on something as long as we feel like it."

"It's a deal."

They toured the farmhouse. Mark and Randy were tangled up together on a mattress in the front room, but everyone else had gone in to town. Jade's list grew longer and longer: a missing doorknob, a window stuck half open, serious leaks around the skylight in the attic, and of course the hole in the bathroom floor. They got a few books from the public library on home repairs, ignored the overdue notices, and by the time the hole in the floor was repaired, they had learned how to replace rotten wood, hang drywall, and plaster.

Jasmine turned out to be the bossy one. Once they got into replacing the bathroom floor, she couldn't wait to get started every morning. Everybody grumbled when she came prowling around the mattresses to drag Jade up from wherever she was sleeping. They didn't like the early morning hammering either. But no one tried to stop them, and Lillian told Jade it was nice to be able to close the door when she put the children to bed.

It was several months before they came to the end of their list. Then the days stretched empty in front of them, with nothing to do but tighten a screw or oil a hinge. Jade took to reading fat historical romances, but Jasmine was no reader. She tried staying stoned, but grass didn't do much of anything for her anymore but give her a headache and put her to sleep.

One evening she was lying on her stomach by the pond at the eastern edge of the farm, teaching Sunshine, Lillian's oldest, how to catch minnows in her fingers. The reflected willows rippled as Sunshine chased the fish. Jasmine gazed back over her shoulder at the house far in the distance, the sky pink and gold behind it like some fantasy of fairyland. As she watched two tiny figures walking back from the barn, she knew what she was going to do.

"Sunshine, we're going to build you a playhouse."

Jade needed no persuading. They sat talking together down by the pond, and the same vision rose to their eyes.

"Up on this slope. We'll make a big window looking through the willows to the pond."

"A kitchen on the east side, with stained glass to catch the morning sun."

"A stairway here up to a sleeping loft...."

"... open on one side so they can watch the stars ...."

"... but screened to keep out mosquitoes."

The dream grew there between them, and Jade wrote it all down, with clumsy sketches.

Now their days couldn't start soon enough. They gathered scrap lumber from miles around, demanded money from Mark for tools and glass. They measured and sawed and hammered, built walls and tore them down again as they saw their mistakes, broke two precious windows before they figured out how to frame them properly. Their friends came down to the pond to watch, but sometimes Jade thought they resented what she and Jasmine were doing, and Mark complained that they didn't want to be part of things anymore. It was true they hardly ever joined the monthly moon dance, and as for sex, during the day they were too busy, and at night they were too beat.

Finally, thirteen months after they first dreamed the playhouse, it was finished. Lillian organized a housewarming. The grownups had to stoop and crouch to wander through the four rooms downstairs, and Jade and Jasmine wouldn't let them up in the loft at all for fear it wouldn't hold them. But it was just the right size for Sunshine and Dakota, and they carried the baby up to the loft to let her try out the hammock. Mark brought his bongos, and William and Alison had flutes. Celia had arrived only the week before with a whole blotter sheet of orange sunshine acid. It was the finest moon dance they had ever known, and for Jade and Jasmine it was especially sweet because they knew it was their last.

The moon set just before sunrise, and people drifted back to the house. Jade and Jasmine sat alone, staring at the dark shadow of the playhouse. The acid was almost spent, leaving them quiet and still. As dawn broke, Jasmine covered Jade's eyes with her hands.

"See what used to be," she whispered. "The bare hill, the willows, the pond. Do you see it?"

Jade nodded her head.

"Now open your eyes."

And there was the little house, lit by the rising sun.

"We dreamed it and now it's there. It came from our heads and our hands. Jade, this is what I want to do."

Fifteen

It was six-thirty when Jasmine came out of the shower. She could hear Jade banging around in the next room. It was coming again, and though Jasmine couldn't imagine what it was like for Jade, she knew how it would be for her. A note on the kitchen table: *I'll be gone for a few days.* And then the house empty except for worry and fear, because although Jade refused to see it, Jasmine knew how dangerous it was. Someday Jade would hook up with the wrong man.

Jade indulged herself in a fling out of town a few times a year. Two or three days in a motel with a strange man she picked up, only Jade and the Lord knew how. The first time it had happened, Jasmine was stunned. The second time, she was furious. The third time, she tried to talk with Jade about it. Why did she do it; what was the point; wasn't it dangerous?

"Where on earth do you get them from?"

"Oh, I just sort of find them, or they find me."

And she was equally, frustratingly vague in all her answers. They went around and around, in a long, tearful weekend, and Jasmine got drunk for the second time in her life. Sunday night Jade was holding her head as she vomited, stroking the hair away from her face. Jade sent her into the bedroom and cleaned up the mess, followed her in with a damp washcloth and clean robe,

111

Jade always came home exhausted from these adventures. Sometimes Jasmine would draw her a hot bath with sweet smelling oils, sometimes she wouldn't speak to her for days, depending on how her fear and anger had worked together that time.

Jasmine went into the kitchen and started the coffee, got the newspaper from the front step. In a couple of minutes, Jade came through the door in her green silk bathrobe, closed at the waist with a leather belt because she had lost the sash.

"Good morning, darling."

A sisterly kiss on the cheek.

Jade sat at the table and unfolded the newspaper.

"Oh, Jesus."

"What?"

"Have you seen this?"

"No."

Jade handed her the front page but went on telling the news.

"The hole's reached the interstate. The southbound lanes have caved in and they've closed them."

"I don't believe it! I thought Dr. Stone told you it was going to stop growing."

"He said he thought it would. I guess it will someday. It can't just swallow the whole world."

"It can as far as I'm concerned, if it will just stay away from the Wilson property."

Jade examined the map in the newspaper. "So far, it's not growing in that direction."

"What do you suppose they're going to do about the interstate?" Jasmine asked.

"I don't see what they can do. It's like Dr. Waites said in that Commission meeting: you can't stop a sinkhole."

"But that's a major highway."

"Yeah, well this is apparently a major sinkhole."

Jasmine brought two cups of coffee over to the table. She squeezed Jade's shoulder, warm and solid under the cool silk, and Jade pulled back. It was definitely coming.

"I'm cooking myself some eggs. You want some?"

"No, I'll just have cereal. I'm having lunch with Clayton Richter today."

"That should be all kinds of fun."

"Don't be bitchy."

"I just don't see why you want to spend time with those assholes. It's not any kind of business lunch, is it?"

"No, but we'll probably talk about the So Long Summer Fair."

"Oh Lord, Jade, are you going to get yourself get sucked into that again this year?"

"What's wrong with it? You said yourself you enjoyed the picnic. And it's good for Opakulla; it brings everybody together."

"Sure, but you did all the work last year and the rest of the Chamber took all the credit."

"That's not true. I had help. And that's how we're going to get accepted in this town, Jasmine. It wouldn't do you any harm to get a little more involved in the community."

"Yeah, maybe I'll go join the Womyn's Freedomsong Church."

"Oh, cut it out."

After they left Harmony Farm, Jade and Jasmine had lived at a lesbian collective for a while. But Jasmine couldn't stand the way everything she did or said became an issue for group discussion. And for Jade it was worse. She spent a weekend away, and they found out she'd been with a man. When she came back there was a long night of interrogation and analysis. They let her stay on because the owner of the house was in love with Jasmine, but Jade was a pariah, and within a few weeks they knew they had to leave. The women at Freedomsong Church were the same, talking endlessly about every little thing, and they were fiercely political on top of it.

If she'd been lesbian instead of bi, Jade could have fit right in. She loved political fights; she loved anything that involved committees and meetings. Instead she had joined the Business Women's Network and the Chamber of Commerce. She said it was good for business, they needed the connections, but Jasmine knew she would have found her way into committees and meetings even if they had inherited a fortune and never had to work for a living.

After they'd been in Opakulla a couple of years, the twins had bought a house on the north side. It was in a little shabby neighborhood near Main Street that was just beginning to become trendy, filling up with artists, writers, musicians. Some of the young faculty at Opakulla University had moved in too. The sisters loved the old-fashioned kitchen, the little octagonal tiles on the bathroom floor, and especially the fireplace. The neighbors welcomed them, invited them to block parties and neighborhood watch meetings, sought their advice about dry rot and leaky windows, hired them for small repair jobs. Finally, they had a place they belonged, and they felt they were home.

Then JJ Visions got the Wilson Trust contract, and suddenly, they lost most of their friends. Home-made signs appeared in the neighbors' yards: *Save the Marsh. No Condos in the Marsh. Stop JJ Visions,* and after Gerald Stone brought all the advocates together, a sign from a printing company, *Friends of the*

Marsh. Jade still had the people she knew from the Chamber and Kiwanis, but she never invited them to the house. Jasmine wasn't really interested in those people anyway.

Jasmine had picked up her guitar and started singing again. She found three women who were looking for a fourth, and they played at free concerts in North Park. She missed the days when she and Jade had the same friends, missed the sense of belonging in the neighborhood. But at one of the concerts she met Claudia, who came up to her at the break and offered her a beer. They started seeing each other, and it became pretty serious. But eventually Claudia began nagging Jasmine to move in with her. She didn't like Jade.

"Love me, love my sister, Sweetheart."

Jasmine said it lightly, but to her surprise, it quickly became the fight that ended it between them.

"You go ahead and love her, Jasmine. She's not my type."

"What do you mean by that?"

"Oh come on, it's obvious what's going on with you two."

"You can't mean…really Claudia, she's my sister."

"Don't worry, I won't tell anybody."

"For heaven's sake, there's nothing to tell. We're twins, I love her more than anybody, but not that way."

"Keep telling yourself that. I'll see you around."

From then on, Jasmine mostly stayed celibate. Lovers were just too much trouble, and she knew how to please herself.

Sixteen

Jade had studied the sky outside her bedroom window before she got dressed and had chosen a wool blend suit. But March was always tricky. By 11:30, when she left her office to meet Clayton downtown, the temperature was over eighty, and the silk lining in the sleeves was sticking to her arms.

It was two blocks from the parking garage to Clayton's office. Passing the plaza, she saw a small gathering of people holding signs. She was early, and anyway, Clayton could wait. He'd probably keep her waiting when she got to his office.

She walked into the plaza. Eleven men and women, in loose robes the color of oatmeal, were walking slowly back and forth in front of the entrance to the Commission building. "Children of Gaia," said the signs they carried, "Don't Rape Our Mother." A policeman watched stolidly from his post at the door, dark patches of sweat on his shirt. She had never seen these people before, but she had heard of them. They lived on a farm south of Missitucknee, growing grapes and blueberries. The Children of Gaia were too pure to collaborate with any other environmental groups, and in their monthly newsletter, Mother Gaia Speaks, they directed most of their wrath at the Nature Conservancy and the Sierra Club, calling them sell-outs.

She walked closer and sat down on one of the benches. Now she heard a soft keening coming from the group—a deep rumble from the men, a high wail from the women. Though she couldn't find a tune in it, they all kept pitch together. The tallest of the men, with long hair and a dark blonde beard, broke away from the circle and walked to the fountain, where he stood with the water leaping behind him. The others stopped their pacing and faced him, still giving forth their wordless crooning. In a deep, strong voice he recited:

Unfathomable,
Inexorable,
Sleeping Gaia
Breathes deep,
And lo:
A hole.

The others joined him at the fountain and began their slow walk around it. A woman called, "Oh Gaia, they have stolen your water." Another, "They have drained your fertile swamps."

The bearded man stepped out of the circle again and faced the door of the Commission building.

"Crumble their stones, oh Gaia, let the land reclaim her soul, and your words become holy to the people."

Jade found their theatrics much more entertaining than the earnest speeches of the mainstream groups. She glanced up at the words above the door. It had been weeks since she'd seen them. They seemed to have lost their sparkle, and even—was it possible?—some of their curves. Now they looked more like the plain, square lettering on ancient monuments. The Children of Gaia trailed back to their line in front of the entrance and began their pacing once again. "Lo: a hole," thought Jade, and smiled. It sounded like a lunch special at the China Garden.

—•—

Clayton Richter had a colleague with him. Brantley Hayes was a young man, not yet easy in a suit and tie, but already developing jowls and a self-satisfied look. Clayton was the senior partner in Opakulla's biggest accounting firm, and this boy was a new associate. He laughed at Clayton's jokes. Sometimes he laughed when there was no joke, and then Clayton glared at him.

They had lunch at the University Golf and Tennis Club. Clayton was a member. Jade was not. No unmarried woman had ever received the three endorsements required to join. Jade didn't like to go there, but she was embarrassed to make a fuss. She couldn't say anything without implying that she disapproved of Clayton's membership. She hated to seem self-righteous.

Besides, she could hear the precise tone, jovial and fatherly, in which he would say, "Oh, now, Jade, you're not going to pull that women's lib stuff on me, are you? You know I'm always the first to see to it that women get a fair shake. After all, I've got daughters of my own. But you know, the Club is still run by the older generation. We'll change things when we take over."

Funny how clearly she could hear him, though she'd never raised the issue. But it was in the way he'd made such a fuss when she and Jasmine first set up shop, the way he'd welcomed her into his office when she approached the firm to see about a retainer arrangement.

"Of course, I don't usually handle the smaller clients myself, but it's not every day we have women entering the construction field."

If she'd turned on the power, he would have propositioned her, but she'd put up that stony wall. She'd vowed never to play those games in Opakulla. Besides, a businessman in his fifties wasn't what she was looking for. Young construction workers, that was more in her line. Or hippies—hippies knew about making love and gave it due priority. The gold-bearded man out there with the Children of Gaia. But his glance had passed over her with no response. He couldn't see beneath her suit.

The time had come for a trip out of town. For months at a time, she didn't think about sex, or, rather, she firmly pushed the thoughts away. And then one day, for no apparent reason, she would find herself noticing eyes, lips, hands, bottoms. Sometimes she was attracted to a woman, but that always ended up emotionally messy. The women she met wanted real relationships, and she was only looking for hot sex. Partnership, intimacy, understanding, love – she had those already with Jasmine, so she limited her honey hunt to men.

She would travel to Jacksonville or Orlando and check into a motel. If she arrived in the evening, she went to a bar, but there was something pack-like about the men in a bar. When she left with one of them, she felt as if he had made a conquest. She'd rather walk into some small coffee shop on a Saturday morning, or a rainy weekday when the construction crews were idling over a second cup of coffee. Her eyes would pick out one man, and then—she'd never been able to explain it. It was as though she sent out a signal, a signal so clear and strong that one time the chosen man came over to the counter where she was sitting and said, "I'm Mitch Fuller. Was there something you wanted?" And that was one of the very best times. For two-and-a-half days he acted as if she had given him a once-in-a-lifetime gift, and they celebrated together.

Now, at the University Club, she ordered a crab salad and sweet tea. She knew why she was here. It was time to start planning the So Long Summer Fair. Jasmine was right, she'd end up doing all the work, but this year she would certainly be chairman. Clayton wasn't ready to talk about that yet, though.

"I want to tell you about an idea I've had, Jade. We have a little gold mine in our own backyard, and we haven't done anything about it."

"What gold mine is that?"

"It's the writing on the Commission building. Market that right, and we can turn it into a tourist attraction, catch some of those people on their way to Disney World, get them off the interstate and have them spend the night here."

"From the paper this morning, it looks like we may not have an interstate much longer."

"We're working on that. The Commissioners won't do anything so we're going to have to get the governor involved. Powell Masterson put in a call to him yesterday, and he's promised to come down the end of the week and make an official visit. He thinks we may be able to get some federal disaster money and put the state engineers on it."

"You think they can stop the sinkholes?"

"Of course they can. Have you been listening to those eggheads at the university? They're smart, don't get me wrong, I'm sure they understand these things in theory, but it happens every time: ask them to actually do something and they don't have a clue. Anyway, what do you think of my idea about the writing?"

"It's very interesting. You're not going to take it on yourself, are you?"

"No, I've talked to Wallace and Cates. They think they can develop a marketing campaign real fast, and they'll do it for nothing. They've been angling for the Chamber's community service award, you know, so they were easy."

"Have you seen the Children of Gaia?"

Clayton frowned. "Yeah, we'll have to get rid of them."

"What are you going to do, cast a spell?"

"Maybe we should just blow them away."

That was Brantley. Clayton ignored him.

"That tall one seems to be the leader. I was talking to someone over at the courthouse the other day who says he's way behind in his child support. I think we can probably get him locked up for a while—no way that group's going to be able to raise the money to pay it off."

It wasn't until the dessert cart came around that Clayton brought up the subject of the fair.

"You did a wonderful job with that last year, Jade. We've never had attendance so high, and the fireworks went off without a hitch. That's actually why I wanted to have lunch with you today. Brantley here is going to be in charge this year—we're planning to make him chairman of the committee, and I wanted you two to get together early on. You can be an enormous help to him, with your experience and all."

She sat stunned. It was obvious that Clayton didn't have a clue what he was doing. Would he care if he did?

What could she say? *Clayton, I don't understand why I'm not going to be the chairman.* It would sound petty. She knew it would come out in a whine. *Fuck your fireworks.* That would be interesting. No one ever seemed to get angry in the Golf and Tennis Club. But it would finish her with Clayton, with the Chamber.

"I'll be happy to help." She said it, and felt her face go hot, a tiny pain start behind her eyes.

121

Seventeen

Tyler passed the Commission building every day now on his way to the office. No matter how early he rode by, the Children of Gaia were already at the fountain. Their daily appearance was almost as mysterious as the letters. Today he stopped to watch them, balancing on his bicycle with gentle taps of his toes.

Every time he saw the letters, he found them changed. Sometimes they were like dark shadows. Sometimes they looked like inlaid golden wires. They were curved or angular, ornate or plain. The Children of Gaia, on the other hand, never changed. Their chant, their slow walk, their clothes. What did they live on? Why did they dress that way?

He stayed awhile longer, enjoying the heat of the sun through his thin cotton shirt. Tomorrow, he and Carol were going to go hiking in the Marsh, this time without the children, who were staying with their father for the weekend. Tyler liked these weekends best. He was growing fond of the children, but the time alone with Carol was precious to him. He'd never understood other people's obsession with sex until he began sleeping with Carol. Now, everything made him think of the feel of her body, the smell of the folds in her skin. The first time was a couple of weeks after their picnic. He plunged into her flesh, soft and warm, almost steamy, and it seemed infinite. She moved and turned under his hands. Each place she touched became in that moment the right place.

In bed and out, he felt completely at ease with her. She was set so solidly in her own self. He felt no falseness, no effort to shape herself to suit him.

When he asked her to go hiking, she said, "I've never done any real hiking, and in this heat, I just don't know. But I'll give it a try."

"Hiking is just a glorified walk. And there's a place where Cypress Creek widens. We can swim there if you like."

"With the snakes and gators?"

"The gators don't hang around the Creek, and we'll watch out for snakes."

—•—

When he picked her up the next morning, Carol was wearing shorts. She looked delicious, and reluctantly he recommended that she change into jeans.

"We're going to be doing some pretty rough walking."

"Now Tyler, I told you I'm not much of a hiker."

"There's no climbing or anything. It's just that we may be going through some brambles, and there's always mud."

"Well, this sounds like all kinds of fun."

"I hope you'll like it. If you don't, I promise I'll never ask you to go again."

—•—

Tyler parked at the beginning of the three-mile Cypress Creek trail. It was closed to the public, but Tyler always had access. Though the day was already hot, there was still a bit of breeze left over from March. The wildflowers were dazzling: flame-blue morning glories, phlox in every shade of pink, and tiny yellow flags.

Tyler was used to walking alone. His own steady pace was hypnotic, and sometimes he would get lost in thought, with no sense of his surroundings. But Carol never settled into a rhythm in her walk. She switched from a stroll to a stride with no apparent reason, stopped suddenly to stare up into a tree at something moving. It was a new experience for him. Still, she didn't chatter, which was something he had secretly worried about. At a muddy patch, where a creek would reappear when the summer rains began, she watched Tyler walk gingerly across bits of dry crust, and then took a flying leap across the middle, missed, and sank to her ankles in mud. Laughing, she reached out her hand for rescue. It was disconcerting, the way she treated it all as play. It was almost like hiking with children, and he said so.

"Honey, it's *nothing* like hiking with a kid, I promise you. 'Are we almost there?' 'I'm hot.' 'My feet hurt.' 'Why did we have to go on this dumb walk anyway?' That's like hiking with a kid. But you forgot to give me hiking lessons. Go ahead and tell me the right way to do it and I'll give it a try."

And she stood in front of him, arms at her sides, a sudden cartoon of a new recruit waiting for orders.

"This is the nicest hike I've ever done. I love you."

It was out before he thought, and he found he didn't mind. When he said it, it became true. She turned away from him and walked on. Tyler followed, watching her bottom. He couldn't understand how she had managed to get mud that high up.

With all the stopping, it took them an hour and a half to reach the swimming hole. Tyler had never seen anyone else there—as far as he knew, it was only known to him and the rangers—so they hadn't brought bathing suits. Carol laughed at him when he turned his back to unzip his pants.

"Do you have something in there I haven't seen?"

He turned around again and she was already half naked, leaning over to untie her shoes before she could get her pants off.

Tyler went in first, balancing on a submerged log and diving for a deep spot. Carol stood a few feet from the edge, looking dubious.

"What's the bottom like?"

"Kind of mucky. You can avoid it if you want. Just climb out on that tree." A long branch stretched a dozen feet across the water. Carol lay down and pulled herself along it to the end, then stood up and jumped in.

The water was warm on top, cool beneath. It was tannic from the cypress, so their bodies slipped in and out of sight, orange as they neared the surface, disappearing entirely as they sank.

Carol lay on her back, her breasts and belly floating above the water.

"What do you think?" asked Tyler.

"I love it."

They stayed in long enough to cool off.

"How are we going to get out? I don't want to walk through the muck now that I'm all clean."

"I'll go out on the branch and haul you up if you want."

"I think I weigh more than you know."

"Maybe I'm stronger than you know."

"Okay, Superman, let's try."

Tyler waded out through the muck, dark clouds swirling up with every step. He pulled on his clothes, sticky and uncomfortable on his wet skin, but better than scraping naked along the tree branch. He inched out the branch on his belly, and wrapped himself around it, reaching one arm down to Carol, who was treading water below. Stretching as far as he could, he was able to grab her by the wrist. Her weight increased rapidly as she rose out of the water and he lost his grip. She fell back in with a great splash.

"Never mind, Tyler. I'll walk out."

"No, no, I can do it. You just need to grab onto my wrist when I've got you—that way we'll both be holding on."

This time he shifted around so he could grab with both hands, keeping his legs tightly twined around the tree. Carol tried to jump, but she had nothing solid to jump against, and instead jerked her arm down as he held her wrist. He lost his hold on the tree and rolled into the water on top of her. She came up laughing.

"I think I'll do better with the muck. But if I ever want to try drowning, I'll be sure to give you a call."

Tyler hung his pants up to dry and they sat naked on his poncho, eating the sandwiches and candy bars he had brought. When they had finished eating, he leaned over on her and she sank under him again. They rolled off the poncho onto the leaves, damp and dappled on the ground. Her skin was still cool, but inside she was warm. Afterwards she dozed off. Tyler wondered how she could sleep there naked on the hard ground, oblivious to the poking sticks and leaves. One had stuck to her hair, and he nudged it off and then kissed the soft wet hair beneath, smelling of tannin and swamp.

They picked each other clean and checked for ticks before dressing.

"Do you want to walk over to the sink hole, or start back?"

"How much farther is it?"

"I'd say it's just under a mile, so that would give us almost four miles back to the car."

"I'd like to see it. Let's give it a try. You can always carry me out if I can't make it."

"I'd have to float you out."

Tyler was amazed again each time he saw the sinkhole. They approached it from the north, near what had been Great Cypress Island, now a long mound in the lake bed. They stood quiet for a minute, close to the rim of the hole. It was eating away at the very edge of the island now, and the roots of some of the ancient cypress were exposed. The sink stretched out in front of them, farther than they could see, deep in some places, shallow in others. The dried lake bed was almost black, and the rest was yellow clay streaked with gray. The whole bowl was littered with fallen trees and shrubs, chunks of clay, white sand.

"What a mess," Carol said. "It looks like some giant demolition. Let's explore."

It wouldn't be safe to walk through the middle. New sinks were forming all the time. They started picking their way around the edge.

Their progress was slow. Carol seemed oblivious to the scratching branches and brambles. At a sudden sharp, cracking sound from behind, they both turned to look. For a moment everything was still, but then the top of a cypress on the edge of Great Cypress Island began slowly swinging through the air in a smooth downward arc. One minute it had stood there for eternity; the next minute, a slight shift of sand, perhaps a single grain, and it fell. It seemed to take forever. Time was frozen, and the crack and crash couldn't break the dream-silence around it. Carol's hand was in Tyler's.

"We were here when it happened," she whispered, and he saw the wonder in her face.

—•—

At Vernell's there was no clear division between the breakfast rush and the lunch rush, but Tyler and Carol arrived at 2:30, after both rushes, starving. There were no cars in the lot, nobody inside. The room was filled with dusty afternoon light, like sun filtered through tall trees.

"Vernell? Are you open?" Tyler called.

No response.

Despite her hunger, Carol would have been happy to trade lunch for a long hot bath. "Maybe we should go."

"Let's sit down. She'll probably be out in a minute," Tyler said, and chose a corner table.

Carol picked up the laminated menu. It hadn't changed since she was a child. And as when she was a child, she wanted everything on it. Mostly, right now, she wanted the coffee she smelled.

"Do you think we could get ourselves a cup?"

"I wouldn't dare. I don't think anyone goes behind that counter."

Carol had always loved Vernell's. When she and her mother opened the door, it felt like they were entering a story book. Maybe it was the mural. She had studied every inch of it, but she always saw something new. This time there was a gap among the cypresses—surely that hadn't been there before. And one of the eagles—was that a snake in its mouth?

Carol sensed something. She turned, and there was Vernell standing in the door that led to the back. She stood still and silent, watching them, and then suddenly swayed slightly, stretched out an arm as if to steady herself, and fell to the floor.

Quickly, Tyler crossed the room and crouched beside her. Carol went behind the counter for a glass of water. Vernell sat up, shaking off Carol's hand on her shoulder. Her eyes opened but she didn't seem to see them. Her mouth moved as though she were struggling to speak. Wordless sounds emerged.

"She's had a stroke. We should call 911," Carol said.

"Wait. Listen."

It was a song, a chant, in no language they knew, and like a dream of waking, it held them motionless. It seemed to go on for hours, but when it was over, the clock assured her that only ten minutes had passed since they arrived. Vernell stood up, smoothed her caftan, and quickly went behind the counter.

"Is that Carol Sperling? I haven't seen you since you were a child."

"It's actually Carol Willoughby now. I changed my name when I got married."

"I don't have to ask what you two have been up to. If I hadn't known you so long, I wouldn't let you come in here looking like that. You can clean up in the bathroom while I get your lunch. I have the bean soup you used to like Carol, and you can have a sandwich—tuna salad or ham. I only have one piece of cobbler left, you'll have to share it."

"But Vernell. Shouldn't we get you to the doctor?"

"Stop your fussing, Tyler. I been uneasy all morning. I have these spells. They're nothing. You go on now, Carol, wash off that mud."

Carol filled the bathroom sink with hot water and squirted in the liquid soap. She paddled her hands to make bubbles, and steam rose to her face with the smell of pine, jessamine, mucky peat. It was delicious, disgusting, intoxicating. She stared into the bubbles. In their iridescence, tiny pictures flashed past like a slide show—a heron, a gator, a slithering snake; the animals appeared and vanished almost before she could name them. Finally, she looked up, the walls fell away, and she saw again the cypress falling. Then it was over. The bubbles were just soap. She washed her face and arms, dried off with a paper towel.

When she came out, Tyler said, "You were in there a long time. Are you all right?"

"Something happened."

"I'll warm your soup up, yours too, Tyler—you go on in and wash up."

The door closed behind him and Vernell sat down with Carol.

"You saw it fall."

"Vernell, we did, and then there in the bubbles…and I saw it again. What happened? What's happening to me?"

"You're all right. I make that soap, and it acts funny with some people. And when the tree fell—you caught some magic."

"I don't understand…how did you know…?"

"Never you mind about that. I know something else too, Carol. You two brought love in here. Maybe you had a vision, but you don't see what's in front of your eyes. That Tyler, he's a good man, and you got no business breaking his heart."

Carol felt like a six-year old. She'd always been a little afraid of Vernell. When you were scolded by Vernell, you stayed scolded.

Tyler came out with his hair wet, looking more rabbity than usual. Nothing seemed to have happened to him in the bathroom; he chattered away about plans for the week. Carol was silent. She had a lot to think about.

Eighteen

Marybeth was tired. It was a beautiful day in May, with the hot blue sky of early summer, all the leaves catching the sun, the air so fresh she could almost smell it through the windows. She ought to be out at Wrigley's Fish Camp, but here she was in a Commission meeting again, sitting behind the long table, her pantyhose twisted and itchy, with Larry Williams, Owen LaGrue, Delmar Mann, Ken Kurtz, Jimmie Bess, and worst of all, with Randall.

She didn't know what was wrong with her today. She couldn't bear the thought of a whole afternoon in that cool and dignified room, everybody acting as if they had some sort of power to change things, make them right. Everyone respectful and respectable, everyone saying what they'd said a thousand times before. She could have held the meeting all by herself, spoken everybody's part. Maybe that's what she should do. "Mr. Mayor, respectfully move we adjourn—I'll carry on by myself." No, then she'd still be stuck inside, while they all went out into the glorious day she could just peek at through the damn high windows.

How much longer could she stay in this job? Maybe it was just her period coming, or maybe, Lord deliver me, she was finally getting into menopause. Nice to have an excuse for feeling so crummy, but really she knew it was the emptiness getting her down. Nothing real came within a mile of this room, it was all words and air, air and words. What she wouldn't give to be back in the store selling screwdrivers.

And here she'd left Munro to do it all on his own. He was the one who'd egged her on to run for the Commission, but now he said it just wasn't any fun at the store without her. And it sure wasn't any fun sitting behind this table every other Wednesday afternoon.

Today they were going to hear another report on the sinkhole. Marybeth couldn't believe how that thing was growing. Bad enough when it caved in under I-75; the detour onto 419 was a pain in the neck. Still, the interstate was a federal problem, or rather, it might be Opakulla's problem, but it was up to the feds to fix it.

Now, though, the ground had collapsed under the water main running out to Colonial Heights. Serves them right for building out in the middle of nowhere. It had cost the city a pile to run the water all the way out there, and nobody ever understood how they got the permits. People had talked of kickbacks, but all that was before consolidation, and she didn't have any way of knowing what had really happened. Now the whole subdivision was without water, and here was Wally Gubrious about to tell them what the water department planned to do about it.

When Wally put on a tie, it did something to his brain. They'd been classmates, but he certainly hadn't learned to talk this way at Opakulla High.

"We are operating since Thursday in the emergency mode. Our manner of proceeding at this point in time is to utilize our full authorized powers to ensure the continuance of necessary services to the residents of the affected areas in question. Going forward we may in fact determine that we will be required to request additional resources ...."

She'd had eighteen phone calls from Colonial Heights. The last two were talking about suing the county. The public safety department had barricaded the whole parking lot at the Food King because it was being undermined, and she couldn't figure out what Wally was telling them, or what he was asking them to do.

"Mr. Mayor. May I interrupt the speaker to ask a question?"

"You have the floor, Commissioner Coggins."

"Wally, do they have any water out at Colonial Park?"

"No ma'am."

"What are they doing?"

"Well, ma'am, they're buying bottled water, carrying it in. I understand some of them have gone to stay with relatives."

"Can you fix the water main?"

"Our ad hoc emergency task force, which was formed at the suggestion of Mayor Fairchild two hours after it was first determined that there had been an incident on subsystem 12-B, what you refer to as the water main, ma'am, has made a full investigation of the possibilities for repair, taking into consideration all possible contingencies and the parameters of the problem, and has come to the conclusion that so long as the general geographic area continues to be subject to further sinkhole activity, repair operations cannot be commenced or undertaken. We have recommended to the Mayor that the Commission consider applying to the Governor's office for emergency funding to construct an alternative routing system bypassing sinkhole activity."

Wally went on about possible routes and cost estimates, and Marybeth's mind wandered off again. Wally had once thrown her in the water at the senior week party at Darlene Cooley's house on Horseshoe Lake. She'd never had too much to do with him before that, or taken much notice of him. Funny how she could still feel his long bony arms, and his elbows digging into her ribs. She didn't get mad, and she shrieked just as loud as he wanted—Wally was shy and this was his way of telling her he liked her. But it didn't give her much of a thrill, not the same thrill she got back in junior high the first time a guy threw her in the water, when she was sitting by the side of the swimming pool at the Y's teen party, hoping one of the boys would notice her.

The air conditioning was on too high. The air was chill, thick, and dead. Delmar was making a motion.

"Move that we instruct staff to prepare a petition for declaration of Opakulla County as a disaster area."

"Second."

"Discussion on the motion?"

No discussion. Seven "Ayes" carried it.

"I believe it would be prudent for me to go to Tallahassee to present our petition to the Governor," said Randall.

Marybeth could see that Randall was excited at the idea, and she could picture him up there in the Governor's office. No, he'd probably try to wangle a lunch with the Governor, get his picture taken. Well, let him. She rubbed the skin around her eyes, felt flesh moving over bone, smelled the onion on her fingers, regretted the hamburger she'd had for lunch. She was too old for raw onions. She had to think about digesting them, instead of letting her stomach go quietly about its business.

Important people, that's what Randall liked. His shoulders straightened just the tiniest bit when he got a chance to be with a VIP. And she couldn't help it; at the same time that she laughed at him, she thought it was kind of cute.

She had to start taking him seriously, but it was hard, watching him puff up like a little boy going off on his first hunting trip. He'd sit up there with the Governor, try to figure out what to do about a sinkhole. Neither one of them from Opakulla. In fact, the Governor had only been in Florida fifteen years; he was a lawyer from New Jersey. They'd probably try to stop it again, or maybe they'd turn it into a tourist attraction, like the magic words. Suddenly she longed so strongly for all this to be gone, for Opakulla to slip back into the sixties, when there was nothing but woods and farms west of Montgomery Street.

She looked at the clock: 4:39. She looked at the agenda, five more reports. Munro would be eating dinner alone again.

Selling the Words

Clayton Richter got together with Wallace and Cates, the advertising firm, and soon there were five billboards, starting in Folkston, Georgia. Going to the Magic Kingdom? First see the Magic Letters, *and down at the very bottom,* Opakulla Chamber of Commerce. *And the people driving south on I-75 woke from their highway daze. College students packed six to a car on their way home for the summer, no longer high but just maintaining after fifteen hours of driving straight from Ann Arbor with a half-ounce of weed. Comfortable women with curly grey hair driving Lincoln Continentals with their husbands snoozing beside them. Parents and children on a long weekend from Atlanta, kids good as gold with Disney lying ahead of them. They all intended to drive straight through until they saw the signs. The Days Inn, Best Western, and Econolodge got, not a flood, but a steady trickle of overnight guests, while the Hilton and Howard Johnson's were left high and dry where the sinkhole had forced a detour around their exit.*

Today, Jim and Louise Irving were there with their grandchildren, Emily, age 9, and Jimmy, 14. They had been on their way to a long weekend at Disney World when they saw the billboards. It was Louise who wanted to stop.

"I'd really like to see that, Jim. And we could get up early, be at Disney World in two hours, looks like on the map. I'm afraid the traffic will be awful bad down there this time of day, and I'm getting all cramped sitting in the car so long."

They'd driven six hours from Atlanta, and only stopped once, when Louise insisted, for the sake of the kids and her bladder. Jim hated to stop, liked to drive on through. If it weren't for Louise and the kids, who got to fussing if they sat too long, he could have made it from Atlanta in five hours, and probably to Disney World in another hour and a half. But Louise wanted to stop and see these magic letters along the way.

Jim had read about them in Newsweek. *He couldn't see what was so special. Letters like you see on any monument, and the words didn't make any sense. Smart though, to think of putting up a billboard, drawing people like him and Louise in to stay the night. And they'd spread that rumor that you couldn't take pictures.*

"Jimmy, get down from there. You're going to break your neck."

He was in the crotch of the big live oak, starting to crawl out on a long horizontal branch. Now he stood up and jumped straight down to the pavement. It must have been fifteen feet.

"Stop fooling around, Jimmy. Go stand over there by the fountain with your sister and grandmother, and I'll get a picture of these so-called magic words."

Nineteen

At First United Methodist Marybeth settled into the corner of her pew, not too close to the front, not too far back. Polly McGilvy turned and smiled, then both sank back into their private thoughts. Marybeth liked to get here early and watch everybody coming in. The fuzzy notes of the organ muted the sounds of people rustling and chatting, deepened the sense of peace. Like a warm bath, it soothed her from skin to soul.

Jane was the organist. Marybeth had known her since the fourth grade. She admired her, supporting herself with her music lessons and the little she got from the church. Always busy, never seemed to miss a husband and children.

She opened her program. There was a baptism today, a family she didn't know. She liked baptisms. She leaned to see around the wide shoulders of the man in front of her. He looked familiar but she couldn't recall his name. Yes, there they were, the young mother and father sitting in the first pew, with a perfectly round-headed baby, Jeremy Paul Madlock Jr., sound asleep in his father's lap.

The first hymn was *God Moves in a Mysterious Way,* one of her favorites. For years she had sung in the choir, but when she decided to run for the Commission she knew she would have to give up something, and the choir was the best choice. After forty her voice had gotten deeper and deeper. It settled somewhere between alto and tenor, and now most of the hymns were set about half an octave too high for her. If she sang where she was supposed to, she lost her voice on the high notes. If she went down an octave, she felt the strain in her throat. She had settled on an uncomfortable accommodation, dropping an octave as the melody rose past the middle of the stave. She had been doing it for years and learned to ignore the occasional stare. It wasn't as bad as Malcolm Sweet, who was sitting two pews up. He had a strong, rich voice, but he couldn't carry a tune, so he simply found a note he liked, and stuck to it.

"God is His own interpreter, and He will make it plain." The last notes echoed from the organ, and the pews creaked as everybody sat down at once and waited expectantly for the lesson.

The Old Testament lesson was from Daniel. The reader this week was Lydia Wheaton. She read in a monotone, but even so, Marybeth felt a shiver at the words.

"Immediately the fingers of a human hand appeared and began writing on the plaster of the wall of the royal palace, next to the lampstand."

A whole hand would be one thing, but just the fingers? That was creepy. She could picture them, bent and bony, moving across the wall, the lamp light casting huge distorted shadows. Reverend David must be planning to talk about the writing on the wall down at the Commission building.

Now the children were being called to the front of the church to witness the baptism. David pulled out his little glass bottle of water from the River Jordan to pass around among the kids as he explained to them about baptizing. She loved this part. You never knew what one of the kids might say or do. When

Harlan, her middle child, was five years old, he had dropped the bottle. It broke and soaked his socks with the River Jordan. David was really sweet about it, probably because Harlan was threatening to cry, and he took advantage of the occasion to explain again what made the water so special. Funny thing was, a month later there was another baptism, and David pulled out another identical bottle with identical water. Maybe there was a preachers' store somewhere that sold these things. This time David finished his little lecture without incident. The children saw Jeremy baptized and then filed back to their pews, looking important.

David went to the lectern for the sermon. She always liked his sermons. It was a puzzle to her how he'd start out one place, wander all over God's kingdom, and end up back where he'd started, precisely twenty minutes later. Once or twice she'd timed him. She didn't really mean to, but she'd glanced at her watch when he started, and then couldn't help checking when he stopped.

He began with some historical background. The Book of Daniel was a series of fables, written at a time when the Greeks were profaning the Temple and oppressing the Jews. They pressured the Jews to assimilate, and a lot of them did. David went on and on about Alexander the Great and the plundering of the Temple and Judas Maccabee, and Marybeth got more and more confused. Where did he get all this stuff, how did he know it? And where was he going with it? Sure enough, he was talking about the writing down at the plaza.

"Are we abandoning our traditions, our way of life?"

What was he talking about? Something about the Yankee invaders. The almighty dollar. We sell the land, our birthright. Well, David was born and raised in Savannah, and as far as she was concerned, he was every bit as much an outsider as Randall or any of the others. He was talking about respect for the earth. Sounded like those hippies out on the plaza with their signs and their chants.

"We cannot finally know the meaning of these words. We have no Daniel to explain them to us. But we can look in Scripture for their meaning, and maybe we should take them as a warning. And in the end, as our first hymn today tells us, 'God is his own interpreter and he will make it plain.'"

Well. David attributed the writing to God. She'd heard that Professor Crannock, in the psychology department, was writing an article about something he called mass hysteria. And in the loony letter file she kept in her desk she had one that blamed the Devil. Maybe she'd go over to the plaza after the service and sit with the letters for a while. Though that strange seizure had only come the first time she saw them, still she always felt a certain trembling of the spirit when she passed by.

They came to the last hymn. Her voice was worn out with the effort of switching octaves, so she just stood and listened to the others. "And turn our foes to friends." Randall popped into her thoughts at the line, though she would have liked to keep him out. Church was supposed to be a refuge from all that. She was sorry to have a foe. Oh, there had been people before who irritated her a little, and certainly people she disagreed with, but Randall was different. Everything he represented was a threat to what she loved. And he would sneer at what she loved, she was sure, if given a chance. Did he ever go to church, she wondered? Probably not. None of the young people who had come to Opakulla in the last few years seemed to have any use for God. The First United congregation was mostly white-haired women.

If only Randall would leave Opakulla alone. She didn't object to him bringing in his own ideas, but like most of the newcomers, he wanted to get rid of what was already there. Except, of course, for the big old houses on Whittaker Street. He'd do anything to protect those, crumbling as they were, and if he had his way, put county money into saving them, buy land and pay to move them.

Last year she'd seen one of them being moved. The great dingy white mansion, porch and turret intact, was creeping down Johnson Road, a narrow street lined with small bright-colored stucco houses on either side, paint peeling off most of them, chain link fences and burglar bars for those who could afford them, old people and young men sitting on their own sagging porches watching the house roll slowly by. It filled the whole street and threatened some of the fences. It was a miracle they ever got it around the corner and out onto Main Street. That move, like all of them, was paid for privately, but who knew what it cost the county to forgive six years of taxes and what part Randall had played.

Forgive. She was supposed to forgive her foes, and she'd always found it easy before, but Randall stuck and pricked at her like a sandspur. She couldn't find any way into understanding him. As she sat with her head down, half listening to the final benediction, she prayed to find some peace with him.

Moving slowly forward in line to shake hands with the minister, through the open door she could see the air almost glowing with the heat. It was beach weather. In her high heels, in that hot air, she simply couldn't walk the three blocks to the plaza; she'd have to drive. The car was an oven, and she opened all the windows before she closed the door.

The plaza was empty, except for Paul, who dozed in his wheelchair under a tree. She sat on a bench near him and watched the pigeons. Were there pigeons all over the world? The only time she'd been out of the United States was when she went to a meeting of local government officials in Montreal. That was in her early days as a Commissioner, when she was all eager to learn and, to be honest, wanted a little of the glamour that she had thought would go with the job. The Montreal parks were full of pigeons. But did they have them in Australia? What about Africa or Norway? Probably they could live wherever people lived. People and pigeons and cockroaches, they must all go together. Somewhere she'd read that cockroaches would survive when everybody else was long gone. Maybe Randall.... Well, she hadn't found her peace in church. It would be good to be a Catholic, then you could confess and get it over with, instead of hauling all this guilt around with you.

She hadn't looked at the words yet. She'd deliberately sat down with her back to them, wanting just to breathe a little before she undertook any puzzles. David said they were a warning from God. Now she looked up. That funny trembling was gone, but the words were kind of blurry. If she hadn't known what they said, she couldn't have made them out, except for one line. *"The well runs dry."*

The words were about her. A decision she'd never even started to think about was suddenly made. She wasn't going to run again for the Commission. She didn't have any more to give, hadn't been able to do any good anyway. They would come in wanting to bulldoze two hundred acres, and if you fought them and fought them you could get it down to one hundred. And then that one hundred was gone for good, and they'd be back the next year, asking for the remaining hundred and settling for fifty. No, she was giving up the fight. Somebody else would have to defend Opakulla, or maybe Opakulla would just have to take care of itself.

Right away she could feel the time ticking down. It was almost June, elections were in October. The new Commissioners would take their seats in November, and she wouldn't be with them. Randall popped into her head—was he ever gone?—and she saw him clear as clear. Tall, good-looking, self-important, and no effect on her at all. He was like somebody who might come in her store to buy a hammer, thank you, have a nice day, then vanish from her sight and from her thoughts. All she had to do was go back to her real life, and he lost all his power to upset her.

It was so easy, and there wasn't any question in her mind. It was 12:30. If she went straight home and fixed Munro a little lunch, she could probably persuade him back into bed for an afternoon nap.

Twenty

Carol was soaked with sweat, and so were the sheets under her.

"Tyler, we're going to have to give up making love until the fall."

"Can't do that," he said sleepily. "We'll turn up the air conditioner."

"No, I don't know why, but if it's hot outside, we get all sweaty in bed, even with the AC on. Maybe it just doesn't work very well."

"Or maybe it's some seasonal biological change—humans sweat in the summer no matter how cold it is."

"That doesn't make any sense."

"Are you dry yet? Here, roll back over."

Tyler had the best shoulder for resting her head on, even if his armpit was still a little damp. Now that she was dry, she liked his warmth along the length of her body. Her ear pressed into his shoulder. She could hear the pulse of her own blood, tried matching her breathing to his, soft and slow. From where she lay, she could look out the window and see the handle of the Big Dipper. Tyler hadn't managed to get curtains for his bedroom. He claimed that since the house backed onto woods, nobody could see in. She hunched down when she had to walk by the window at night. She'd thought of making him curtains, but that seemed too committed, too coupled.

Carol was a little sad about their relationship. Here she was, facing Happiness, and she had cold feet. And it wasn't just her feet. Her whole body had frozen up on her, so no matter where Tyler touched her, her flesh was almost numb. Oh, faint sensations followed his hands, his lips, but her heart wasn't in it. Her mind wandered and returned to find him still trailing his fingers down her thigh, and thought, "But that ought to feel so good." "When Randall did it, it felt good," remembered her thighs. "Now don't bring up Randall," her mind would reply crossly. And so she would lie there, quite at odds with herself, while poor Tyler went on feasting and playing, and never had a clue. How could he? At least she could feel enough to have an orgasm, but it was a pale little thing, like weak tea.

From the beginning, she'd known she shouldn't get involved with him. There was something missing, some spark. But she told herself, trying to be adult about it, that she shouldn't judge so quickly. She ought to give him a chance. Besides, there was no harm in having a cup of coffee with a guy. And now she was stuck, like a gnat in honey. Just when she had resolved to call a halt, she would speak of the rest of the summer, or let him make plans for the weekend. It was so nice with Tyler, even if the sex was nothing more than a warm snuggle. It was hard to break it off and go back to the bleakness of nobody. Like getting out of a hot bath on a cold day with no towel to wrap around her.

Had she been leading him on from the very beginning? She'd never said I love you, but he never seemed to need it. She couldn't understand it. Tyler was the nicest man she'd ever known. The comfort of being with him, the absolute fitness when they were together, the way she could tell him anything, never felt he was judging her, or that she had to pretend to be anything she wasn't. The way he admired her—that was the most astonishing of all.

He thought she was smart and told her so. He encouraged her plans for college. He praised her kids, her house, her African violets. Did little acts of kindness—silly things, really. He brought her a glass of water when he was getting one for himself, covered her with a blanket when she fell asleep on the couch. The rose at the hospital. He wasn't embarrassed about loving her, didn't demand that she say it too. He was a thoughtful and enthusiastic lover. So why didn't he turn her on? Maybe the possibility of a real, loving relationship with a nice man froze her blood. It was too discouraging to think about. She grabbed his arm and wrapped it around her, reached down and pulled a sheet up.

"What do you want to do this weekend?" he asked.

"Oh, I don't know. It would be nice if we could find someplace to go swimming besides the city pool."

"Well, we could go out to Murray's Lake. Take a picnic. We could wrap Christopher in a plastic shield for the yellow jackets."

She didn't answer.

"Hey. Carol?"

"That was my fault."

"What was?"

"Christopher's bee sting. That was my fault."

"Don't be silly. What were you supposed to do, grab the wasp before it got him?"

"Not that he got stung, I don't mean that. But I knew he was allergic. I'm supposed to have an injection pen with us for emergencies. The trouble is…."

Her voice got smaller and smaller.

"See, Christopher was a baby the first time he got stung, and I took him to the emergency room and they told me about the pens. I was scared, so I bought one, but it was hundreds of dollars. And then he never got stung, and it expired after a year, and I just didn't see how I could go on buying something that expensive that I never use."

Her face was buried in the pillow by now, and he could hardly hear her.

"Hey. Look at me." He pulled on her shoulder until she rolled over, but she kept her hands over her face.

"Don't cry about it."

She went on crying.

"I'll buy the pen. I can afford it."

"Tyler, you don't understand. I have to do it myself."

Now was the time to explain they weren't some kind of permanent couple. She ought to end it here, but she couldn't right now. Still, she wouldn't let him carry her load. Her load was all she had.

—•—

Tyler lay awake long after Carol had gone to sleep. This was all much more complicated than he had realized. That picture he'd had of the richness of her life, beneath the smooth surface. It wasn't rich; it was just chaotic. She wasn't a weaver, in perfect control. She was more like a juggler with too many balls in the air, and not just balls, but candlesticks, heads of lettuce, eggs, light bulbs, myriad objects in all shapes and sizes. Only natural that she'd let some of them drop, and then scramble to retrieve them.

He himself was one of those objects, he knew by now. She would slip in time with him—an occasional lunch, a picnic with the kids, and a rare whole night when she could arrange the babysitting. But she wouldn't let him spend the night at her apartment, even though the children liked him. She wouldn't even let him pay for the babysitter.

When he called her on a Saturday morning, asked if she'd like him to come over, it was always, "Oh, Tyler, I have a thousand chores."

"I could help you with them."

"No, I don't need help. I'll call you this afternoon. Maybe you could come over for dinner or something."

So he would pick up a pizza to spare her cooking. After dinner they'd watch television with the kids, and after the kids went to bed they'd sneak into her room and make silent love. He'd just be falling off to sleep when she would poke him and say, "Honey, don't fall asleep now, you need to go home."

The drive home was so lonely, and when he got home he couldn't get to sleep for a couple of hours. He was just a temporary visitor, let into the corners of her life. How could he get her to really invite him in? He would ask her to marry him, but what if she said no? He was pretty sure she would; she'd never even said that she loved him. And if she said no, would they be able to go on as they were? Even the little bit that she allowed him was far too nice to give up.

He tried to think back to before Carol. Hadn't that been a tranquil, happy life? Now it was all disruption and longing. Thoughts of her crept in as he prepared his lectures. When he went out of town to a conference, he missed her. Everything he saw made him think of her, and he'd come home loaded with little gifts. He'd buy a book that would interest her, or toys for Robin and Christopher. But something about the way she said, "Tyler, you shouldn't have," sounded all too sincere. She kept him at arm's length, along with all the other things she was juggling, and he was afraid she'd never let him get any closer.

The moon was up now, dimming the stars. He adjusted himself around the warm curve of Carol's back, pressed his mouth against her shoulder, shining in the moon light, and went to sleep.

A Giant Falls

The moonlight woke the shadows on the Marsh, leaving the colors sleeping. Water in the ponds gleamed silver. Trees stood ghostly, and in the deep shadows, pairs of eyes reflected the light.

The night shift was in full swing. Mice scurried through the tall grass, nibbling as they went. The great horned owl dropped from his tree and grabbed a young rabbit, its single shriek cut short as the talons shifted and broke its neck. Restless in the bright moon light, a bull gator gave a great roar, and from his belly sent a deep booming love song through the pond. Drops of water flew into the air around him. A female moved closer to lie, ecstatic, in the vibrations, and all the other gators began to bellow.

The trees of Great Cypress Island shivered. At the top of the tallest, two bald eagles slept. They'd nested there for eighteen years, and their descendants nested near them, in cypress and pines. But now, with a loud crack that silenced the alligators, the tree fell. Still in a half dream, the eagles rose into the air, woke, and sailed away as the giant crashed through the brush onto the dry lake bed.

Chapter Twenty-One

Tyler was giving Carol a puppy for her birthday. He wanted to get her a dog with papers, but she insisted they go to the pound.

"Those purebred dogs have all kinds of problems, Tyler, unless you spend hundreds and hundreds of dollars."

"Well, I don't mind spending the money. That way you can get just the kind of dog you want."

"I don't feel comfortable with you getting me such an expensive present, and besides, what I really want is a mutt. I'm a mutt myself."

They decided to go to the pound with the kids, and on the morning of her birthday Tyler handed her a big brown bag. Carol laughed as she opened it.

"You know, some people would have wrapped it."

"I'm no good at giftwrap."

She pulled out the dog bed, feeding dish, leash, the book on puppy training.

"I see this mutt is going to have nothing but the best."

"Well, you wouldn't let me buy you a purebred. I wanted to get you something nice."

"I promise, we'll get a nice puppy. You wait here, and I'll go downstairs and get the kids."

"Do they know we're going to get the dog?"

"No, I wanted to surprise them. Besides, if it didn't work out, I didn't want them to be disappointed."

"What wouldn't work out?"

"We could have had an enormous fight last night, and you'd have stormed out of the house, and I'd never see you again."

"Can you picture us having an enormous fight?"

"No, and I can't picture you storming, either."

He thought she sounded wistful, but she had turned away as she said it, and he couldn't see her face.

"Do you want me to storm?"

"Don't be silly, Tyler, you are what you are. I'm going downstairs."

Tyler arranged the paraphernalia conspicuously: the dog bed next to the couch, the feeding dish on the floor by the sink, the leash draped over the coffee table.

The children came clattering up the stairs, and Christopher banged the door open.

"Where's the puppy?"

"We don't have him yet, Christopher. Mommy said we're going to go get him, right Tyler?"

"Right."

"I'm going to get a pit bull, man, then nobody can mess with me."

"It's not your dog; it's Mommy's. It's a birthday present for her, and she gets to choose."

"We'll all choose." Carol had followed them up the stairs.

—•—

The pound was out in the middle of nowhere. A woman was leading a dog on a leash from her station wagon to the office.

The dog, a black and tan with bulging wall eyes, was struggling to resist the leash.

"She's a stray. She's been hanging around our house, but we can't keep her," the woman said apologetically to Carol.

"Can we get that one, Mom? Look at him jump. He's doing somersaults."

"Let's look at all the dogs, Chris, before we make up our minds."

The puppies and dogs were in long rows of cages. It reminded Tyler of prison movies, and the clamor was as great. But at least the dogs were out in the fresh air. They were kept two to a cage in odd, random pairs—a dachshund with a giant brindle dog of indeterminate mix, a husky with a little mottled brown terrier. Tyler wondered about fights. The barking followed them down the rows. So did the smell, not strong, but definitely dog.

The puppies were kept in litters, and the children stopped at the first puppy cage. These were sandy brown dogs with floppy ears. They were sleeping, but Christopher took care of that. They staggered out of their pile, blinking and yawning. There were five of them.

"I want that one," said Christopher.

He pointed to a little one, darker than the rest, who stood with his legs planted wide, and challenged them with a tiny fierce bark.

"He's really cute, isn't he? But don't you want to look at all the puppies before we decide?"

"Yeah!" and he raced three cages down.

When Tyler was nine, his father had bought a dog. He bought it for a watchdog, and jealously guarded his training and feeding. Tyler played with the puppy when it was small, but his father insisted he use only the prescribed commands and feed him at exactly the same time every day, and Tyler soon lost interest. Walking down the rows of cages, he thought about choosing a dog for himself. But he was home so seldom, and besides, he could share Carol's dog. They might be living together before the summer was out. Not in her place or his. His was too small for children, and hers was too small for him. He'd started noticing the price of houses. They could afford a good-sized place on just his salary, not even counting Carol's.

There were six cages of puppies. Carol sent Tyler back to the office to find out something about them, but there wasn't much to find out. Only one litter was a clearly identified breed, the product of the meeting of a collie and a pit bull. Carol ruled them out because of the pit bull. Luckily Christopher didn't hear it, and since there were only two puppies in that cage, he seemed less interested in them anyway. They kept coming back to that first cage. This time the fierce male had gone to sleep, and two females were tumbling over each other in a corner.

"Shall we get one of these?"

"Can't we get two? That way they can keep each other company when we're not home."

"No, one puppy will be enough."

"But Mommy, they'll be lonely."

"One puppy, Robin."

"But it's so hard to choose."

"How about that one there, who's chewing on the other one's ear?"

"Yeah, I like him."

"Actually, that's a female puppy, Christopher."

"But I want a boy!"

"We'll be better off with a girl, darling. Other dogs don't want to fight with them as much."

"Get your dumb girl dog then. I didn't want one anyway."

Carol ignored him, and he trailed along behind them to the office, running a stick along the chain link of the pens, setting all the dogs barking again.

When they reached the car, Carol sat in back so the kids could sit on either side of her and pat the puppy. But Christopher wanted to sit up front with Tyler. Robin sat next to Carol, and scratched the dog's ears, murmuring "Nice puppy, nice puppy."

Tyler wondered how she managed to murmur so loudly. Christopher was squirming around in his seat, trying to see over the back. Robin patted more vigorously.

"What do you think we ought to name her, Chris?" Carol asked.

"Daisy," answered Robin.

"That's a dumb name. Let's name her Marmaduke."

"You can't call her that; there's already a dog named that. Anyway, that's a boy's name."

"How do you know? I don't know anyone named Marmaduke."

"It is a boy's name, isn't it, Mommy?"

"Yes, I think it is. I'll tell you what, why doesn't everybody think of three names and then I'll choose."

Robin came up with Honey, Daisy, and Cuddles.

"Let's name her Shitty." Christopher was overcome with his own wit.

"I think not, Christopher. You get two more."

"He already said Marmaduke. He only gets one more."

"No, that's not one. I said that before Mom said we get to choose three, so it doesn't count."

"Well, then I get one besides Daisy."

Carol caught Tyler's eye in the mirror and smiled. "Lawyers."

"You can't name her that, Mommy."

"No, Robin, I know. What's your other name?"

"Rosie."

"What about you, Chris? Do you have your other two yet?"

"Tiger and Duster."

"Tyler?"

"I think maybe you have enough names."

"Okay," Carol said. "I pick Duster."

Christopher gloated. Robin sulked. But Carol let her carry the puppy into the vet's office.

At home, Christopher got to carry her up the stairs. They watched her explore the kitchen, and pee on the floor. They took her down to the backyard. Carol dragged two lawn chairs out from under the house, and before she could sit, Tyler pulled hers closer, right up against his. They sat without speaking, holding hands, watching the three puppies play.

Robin had found a ball. She rolled it to Christopher, Duster scrambling after it, and then Christopher threw it back to her. Duster leaped into the air and fell on her back, lost interest in the ball, and began tracking a smell across the grass. Christopher got on his hands and knees and tracked Duster. Robin went between them, picked up Duster and cuddled her thoroughly.

"Hey, no fair, she wants to play."

Robin put her down and joined Carol and Tyler.

"Mommy."

"What, honey."

"I wish we could get two dogs."

"I do too, Robin, but you know, dogs are a lot of money and a lot of trouble. We're going to have to train Duster."

"What are we going to train her to do?"

"Well, not to pee on the floor, for one thing."

"Who do you think is going to get all those other dogs?"

"Oh, there's lots of other children and their moms looking for a pet."

"What if nobody comes? Do they have to stay in those cages all their lives?"

Carol took her hand.

"They only stay at the pound for ten days, Robin. If nobody wants them, then they're put away."

"Where do they put them?"

"No, that's just a way to say they give them a shot that puts them to sleep, and they never wake up. They die."

"You mean they kill them?"

"That's right."

"That's awful. You mean Duster would be killed if we hadn't of taken her?"

"But Robin, we did take her. You don't need to cry."

"But what about all those others, and they're going to kill her sisters too. Those are bad, bad people."

Robin was up on Carol's lap now, crying freely.

"Sweetie, we can't save them all. All we can do is what we can do. You just take care of Duster and be glad she has a nice home like this with a little girl to love her."

Robin stayed on her lap for a few minutes, sniffling and sucking her thumb, watching Christopher and Duster chasing each other. Tyler watched Carol rocking in the lawn chair, stroking Robin's hair, until she slid down and went to join Christopher.

"It's too hot and sticky out here. Want to go upstairs and have some tea?"

"OK."

"You kids make sure the puppy stays in the yard. Watch that one place where the fence is torn. Be sure she doesn't find it."

—•—

"Why did you tell Robin about the pound?"

"You mean about killing the dogs?"

"Yes."

"She asked me what would happen to them, and I told her."

"You could have just told her they'd be adopted."

"But they won't be, Tyler. I try to tell them the truth."

"I guess you're right. But I wouldn't have had the nerve."

"You think I should have lied to her, don't you?"

"No, I don't think so. Just…there must be some way to soften it."

"Soften what? Life? Life's rough."

It was funny, she thought. Tyler had asked his question because he wanted to know, there wasn't any accusation in it. With Randall…she could hardly imagine a conversation like that with Randall. She always felt an extra edge with him when it came to the kids. He'd never said anything, but she often sensed disapproval of their behavior, of the way she raised them. Even

159

their names. When she first introduced them, "Randall, this is Christopher and this is Robin," he had looked pained.

"It's from Winnie the Pooh you know."

"Yes, I know. It's very cute," he said politely.

But she soon learned that, for Randall, cute meant big plastic Santa Clauses in the yard, teashops with an extra p and an e on the end. He wouldn't go into those *teashoppes*. He wouldn't go with them to see *Fantasia*. Tyler would go with her anywhere. He'd jump at the chance.

"Hey, I'm taking the kids to the dentist next week. Want to come?"

"You're kidding."

Well, maybe not anywhere.

Coming Closer

The sinkhole kept growing in fits and starts. One grain of sand teetered on the rim, slipped, knocked into another and started a tiny avalanche. A clod of dirt rolled down the slope and dislodged other clods. A shift here, a shudder there, a stretch of ground, dry and cracked, sinking in a moment to become a smooth slide of yellow sand. The boundaries crept outward, slide by slide, met smaller sinks and swallowed them. And the bottom of the hole kept sinking.

But the hole was growing westward, away from Cypress Lake. The danger to the Trust land seemed to be over. There had been no activity near that area since the lake disappeared. Jade and Jasmine spent a happy Sunday tying plastic ribbons around the trees they planned to save. No one could have predicted that the sink would suddenly reverse course.

In a monstrous, two-week convulsion, the hole sank deeper and spread east and south. Into the pit fell the trees, beribboned or not. Swallowed up were the birds' nests and spider webs, the shrubs, grasses and wildflowers, the bugs and small beasts, while the bigger beasts scrambled away. On Highway 226, three possums and a bobcat were killed in a single morning, and in town the postmaster caught two deer nibbling on the crape myrtles behind the new post office. A low, steady rumbling was heard in Opakulla, and a cloud of yellow dust hovered over the Marsh.

Chapter Twenty-Two

Carol was excited. Her voice came in little bursts.

"Tyler, there's someone on the phone from Washington. She's with the Terrell Hastings show. They want to talk to you."

"How come?"

"I don't know. She didn't say. I'm going to transfer her to you. I don't want to keep her waiting."

—•—

"Dr. Waites, this is Melissa Lanchester from the *Hastings News Hour.* We're doing a feature this week on the environment, and I'd like to spend some time on your extraordinary sinkhole. They tell me you're the man to call."

"I suppose I am."

Tyler enjoyed talking with her. From somewhere she had already acquired a rudimentary knowledge of geology, and he got quite carried away describing the growth of the new sink. It was a little harder dealing with the meaning of it all, particularly when she challenged him to name the cause.

"Some people think sinks are more common after long spells of drought, when there's no water in the limestone to support the weight above it. Others think a series of wet seasons increases the rate at which the rock gets eaten away by acid from the mulch. We've mapped out several plots of land around this part of the state and we're tracking sink activity and rainfall, among other things. This will be the first measure of sink formation over time. It's very exciting, really, but I've only been doing it for two years, and I don't expect to have much useful data until another dozen years or so."

The office door squeaked open, and Carol poked her head in. He reached out his hand, she closed the door behind her and came and stood close to him.

"Well, I don't think we want to wait that long to do our feature," Melissa Lanchester said. "We're hoping to air it on Thursday, and I wondered if you'd be available tomorrow night."

"Available?"

"WOPA will tape your part of it. They've got a camera crew out at the Marsh this morning, and they said they could take you in the studio at 6:30."

"Oh no, I don't want to be on your show. I'm really not a very good speaker."

"Dr. Waites, you've been talking to me almost fifteen minutes about sinkholes. It was fascinating, and I think you'd do very well on television."

"But I have plans at 6:30."

Both women spoke at once.

"Tyler, for heaven's sake, we can change dinner time."

"I'm sure we can find another time at the studio."

So he gave in. It really wasn't as bad as that time he'd just missed being on radio, when Gerald took over. He didn't know anything about mysterious writing, but he did know about sinkholes. He could talk about the Marsh sinkhole for hours. Melissa Lanchester thought it was interesting, and it was her job to know.

National television. He'd never seen Carol so excited.

"What are you going to wear? You need a blue shirt."

"This is blue, isn't it?"

"Oh, Tyler, you can't wear that old Shop and Save stuff on national TV."

"Why not?"

"Maybe I can take the afternoon off and we can go down to Goldman's and find you a really nice suit."

"Carol, whoa. Slow down now. Number one, I don't want a suit. Number two, my clothes are perfectly fine. What's her name told me who to call at WOPA, and if I need to wear any special colors or anything, they can tell me. It's just not such a big deal as you're making it."

"Well, I want you to look good."

Tyler was enjoying this. She was being so wifely. Was this how it would be if they got married—her taking care of him? Acting as if his business was her business? It was an odd feeling. He couldn't tell yet whether it was odd-nice or odd-awful. On the whole, he liked it, but he realized that there was more to marriage than he'd thought about.

—•—

The show made a bigger stir than Tyler had expected. WOPA called the *Chronicle* to let them know the Marsh sinkhole was going to be featured that Thursday. The *Chronicle* ran a big story on the front of the second section with a picture of Tyler that Carol gave them. Lucille Harroway called Tyler and invited him to come watch the Hastings show with them and a few of their friends. He declined. He'd never met the Harroways, and besides, he and Carol were going to watch it with the kids.

—•—

He sat in the corner of the couch with Carol leaning against him. The couch, which had already absorbed nine years of every type of human juices, was now subject to Duster, who piddled when she got excited. Tyler thought perhaps they could replace it when they moved.

Robin and Christopher were on the floor with their legs stretched out under the coffee table. Christopher was picking the pepperoni off his pizza and laying the circles in a row on the lid of the box.

The narrator's voice rumbled like God's as the camera moved over the waters and valleys. For a good ten minutes he mourned the devastation wrought by man. The children were restless; they were trying to get Duster to do tricks for Christopher's pepperoni.

"Robin, pepperoni isn't good for her," said Carol. "Oh, look, there you are."

It was funny to see himself on television. His voice was higher than he'd realized. His eyes almost disappeared behind his glasses. Carol's television had seen better days, though not while she owned it. From time to time his face slid up the screen, followed by his face, which slid up the screen, followed by his face again. Sometimes the picture hovered, with his nose and chin hanging from the top and his forehead and eyes coming up from the bottom.

The sound was fine, though, and Tyler was pleased with his five minutes. He had explained the sinkhole clearly, he thought, without simplifying it too much.

His segment closed with an aerial view of the sink. Although he had been measuring it for weeks, Tyler was astonished to see its full size all at once. It had swallowed almost a quarter of the Marsh. The hole could have been a giant bomb crater. A thin ribbon of road, the interstate, ran up to the edge and stopped, resuming on the other side.

"You were wonderful. But next time you need to watch out for your eyes. You kept gazing up and it looked a little odd."

"I guess that's what I do when I'm thinking."

"We can practice with the camcorder at the department so you can see yourself."

"Carol, I'm not planning on going into television."

"Oh, I think once those news people discover you as an expert, they keep coming back. This could be really good for your career."

"Honey, television appearances don't have anything to do with my career. I didn't mind it this once, but I'd be just as happy never to do it again."

She brought her mouth right up to his ear and whispered, "I think you're real sexy on television. You do the kitchen, and I'll get the kids to bed."

She said it so casually, as if they shared the chores every night. But it was the first time he'd felt like more than an interloper at Carol's place. Usually she sat him down in a corner while she cleaned up the kitchen, supervised baths, read the bedtime stories. He'd learned to bring a book with him for those times, and he'd lie back obediently with his shoes off and his feet up on the couch when she told him to relax. But he always felt trapped on the couch, awkward and out of place, forbidden to take up more than his allotted space. His knees stayed stiff, and he couldn't get his feet to lie right.

The pizza dinner hadn't made much of a mess, but there were the dishes from breakfast and lunch, and innumerable glasses. He wanted to make everything sparkle, show her how useful he could be. He never thought he'd be courting a woman with housework. He never thought he'd be courting a woman, period. He hadn't understood how complicated it could be. Carol wasn't just going to come along and join him on his path, fill the little hollow in his heart. There were all these pieces they'd have to fit together, like a jigsaw puzzle.

—•—

When Tyler arrived at the office the next morning, Carol already had five phone messages for him. Lucille Harroway, the Hastings show, someone from the *Chronicle*, and two people he couldn't identify.

"I don't want to call all these people."

"It's the price of fame, Dr. Waites." Carol held her smile in check, except around the eyes.

He was working on a paper for the San Francisco meeting at the end of July. There was a fresh data run piled up on his desk, and he'd been looking forward to digging through it. He decided he'd call them back in the afternoon, when he'd done all he could do on the paper.

As he was unlocking his office, Gerald came by. Tyler hadn't seen him since the phone call from Melissa Lanchester. He hadn't had a chance to tell him about the television show.

"Hello, Waites. I understand you were on television the other night. Sorry I missed it."

His voice was low and toneless, and Tyler could swear he was smaller than the last time he'd seen him, as if his chest had deflated. He kept moving down the hall and into his office.

Surely Gerald couldn't be jealous. Should he have recommended him for the show? But Gerald didn't know very much about sinkholes. Of course, he hadn't known much about the writing on the wall either, and he'd been happy to talk about that. Still, sinkholes were definitely Tyler's territory. And Gerald didn't seem angry. He seemed depressed. What could be bothering him? Tyler went into his own office and shut the door, heading straight for his new data.

Chapter Twenty-Three

Carol spotted the card on Tyler's hall table, sticking out from the clutter of bills and old mail.

"What's this?" She picked it up to see.

"Oh, an invitation to some party. I guess I ought to answer it."

"Tyler, this isn't just some party. This is the Harroway's Fourth of July dinner at the Golf and Tennis Club. I didn't know you knew them."

"I don't."

"They must have seen you on TV. Their parties are wonderful. All the important people in town are there. I went to one once when I was going with Randall."

"Actually, they invited me over to watch the TV show with them."

"And you didn't go?"

"Of course not. You know I didn't go. I was watching it with you and the kids."

"Well, I know, but you can be with us anytime."

"Why would I want to go watch myself on TV with people I don't even know?"

"You'd get to know them; it would have been perfect, probably just a few people."

He took the invitation from her.

"You're going to want to go to this, aren't you?" His voice was glum.

She almost said yes, but she could feel the sand castle crumbling, grief rushing in even before the conscious thought— she and Tyler couldn't go on together. Something was missing in him. That he could turn away from the world she wanted, that was just a piece of it, but it was a part that made the rest clear to her, forced her to see what she'd been trying to ignore.

He was perfectly self-contained, needed no one's approval or admiration. He lacked the rooster's strut, the lion's roar. And all of it meant male to her, so she would lose everything she had with Tyler, the comfort, the friendship, the understanding. Why couldn't he be what she needed him to be? Why did she demand that this good man be what he wasn't?

There was something wrong with her. He was just what the children needed, Christopher especially. He was so much calmer, so much nicer, since Tyler had started hanging around. She would throw all that away, and for what? She knew the men that were out there, none of them worth half of Tyler.

He was going to ask her to marry him soon, she knew that. And he'd take her to the party if she wanted; he'd go anywhere she asked. But he couldn't make that spark between them, the spark that led sometimes to anger and sometimes to sex.

"Hey, Carol, what's wrong?"

She was just standing there, staring at him. She shook her head slightly and groped for a chair, sat at the table with her head in her hand. Now she wouldn't look at him.

"Carol, honey. We can go to the party. I don't mind."

"It's not that."

"What then?"

"It's not going to work."

"What won't work?"

But she could tell that he knew and wanted to stop her from saying it. She wouldn't stop, though she spoke softly, as if it would hurt him less.

"Tyler, it's you and me. We don't belong together."

"Of course we do."

"No. It's not right between us."

"But what's wrong? We get along together so well. I've been so happy. I thought you were too."

"I was, I mean I am."

"Is it something I did?"

"No, you didn't do anything, damn it, Tyler, there's nothing I can tell you except it just isn't right for me."

They sat at the table. Carol looked down at her fingernails. Tyler looked at Carol. After a while of nothing but their breathing, he spoke.

"I was going to ask you if you wanted to live together."

"I know you were."

She was wondering how long she had to stay there with him. Her whole face was tight with the effort not to cry. She wouldn't cry now. Just sit and fiddle with her nails until he dismissed her.

"I wish…." He looked at her. Her face was so hard and angry he couldn't go any further. "I guess there's nothing more to say."

"Guess not." She waited, but he was silent. "I'd better be going."

Out the door, fresh air, thank God she could breathe again, relax. But as soon as she let her body relax, the pain came. This was the worst it had ever been. It wasn't like losing someone she wanted passionately. She'd done that often enough. No, this was worse. The revelation that even when she understood what she was doing, even when she saw plainly what was good for her and the kids, she couldn't reach out and take it. As if she'd been lucky enough to come upon a flower growing in her yard, and had yanked it up, roots and all, and thrown it away. She'd never find a man as nice as Tyler. Why hadn't he insisted, been more forceful, fought to hold on to her? Because then he wouldn't be Tyler.

Her future looked so grim. The best that could happen would be that she'd avoid men altogether. But that was unlikely. She'd never spent longer than three months between lovers. No, she'd probably go on hooking up with guys who weren't right for her, guys who tried to boss her around, who looked down on her. She didn't see any way out.

—•—

The next morning, Tyler sat in his kitchen. It was small and windowless, with a single counter and a round table for two. He fiddled with a coffee stirrer. The television was on, but he didn't watch it. Instead, he was watching the clock, waiting for 8:00, so he could call the office. He knew Carol would answer, and he needed to hear her voice. Finally, the big hand clicked over the twelve and he dialed.

"I won't be in the rest of the week."

"Are you sick?"

"No, I'm going to stay home and work on my paper for San Francisco."

"OK."

"Well, goodbye, I guess."

"Goodbye."

He sat with his hand on the receiver. Everything seemed to be in slow motion. It took effort even to breathe, and he wasn't sure it was an effort worth making. He had waited so eagerly to hear her voice, but her voice hadn't offered him anything. And now the rest of the day stretched out in front of him. Piled on the table were a bunch of journals, but there wasn't any point in reading about karst formations in Eastern Europe.

Tyler had never been through this before. He was shocked by the storm of sorrow he was caught in, and outside the tempest, nothing. How could he work with this gripping, paralyzing pain? It never occurred to him that he might try to change her mind. She knew what she wanted, and it wasn't him. Why did he ever get involved with her anyway? He'd been perfectly content before she came along. If he'd had any idea what this loss would be like, he never would have risked it. But he hadn't seen the risk. He had been puzzled, it's true, by her holding back the way she had. But their friendship had grown so smoothly and pleasantly, never a quarrel, always enjoying each other's company, none of the torment of uncertainty. Well, he was getting the torment now.

—•—

"The Lord makes us humble before he takes us home."

Tyler pushed open the screen door further, and Vernell looked over at him. She was in her rocking chair again, talking with Jared. She looked tired.

"We missed you yesterday, Tyler. I was just telling Jared about my Momma."

173

Tyler knew that Vernell's mother lived with her and kept a big vegetable garden going in their backyard. Sometimes Vernell put fresh tomatoes on their breakfast plates.

"The doctor says she needs an operation, and then she won't be able to go to the bathroom by herself. I never thought she'd get that way. And I don't know how I'm going to take care of her."

"Don't you have some family that can help?"

"My sisters, we'll work it out somehow, with the Lord's help. You ready for your coffee? You're so late this morning; Jared's about finished his breakfast."

"I'm working at home this week. Have to finish a paper."

She gave him a sharp look.

"That don't mean you can go without your breakfast."

Jared folded his paper napkin neatly and put it next to his plate.

"If you'll excuse me Tyler, I have to get to work. Thank you, Vernell. I hope your mother will be feeling better today."

When Vernell had put Tyler's breakfast in front of him, she sat back down in her rocking chair, where she rocked steadily, watching him as he ate. Under her gaze, he couldn't finish his grits. He wasn't very hungry anyway.

"Lost your appetite, Tyler?"

"It's been awfully hot."

"It's not the heat troubling you."

And so Tyler found himself telling her all about Carol.

She rocked and listened.

"I thought you had something going on the last few months. Sorry to see it gone. You think you can get her back?"

"No. I can't very well go begging her."

"More men's hearts broken through pride; you don't see women acting so foolish."

"No, Vernell; I think Carol knows what she wants, and it isn't me. She used to go out with that Commissioner, Randall Fairchild. She said some terrible things about him; I don't think he ever treated her very well, but I have a feeling he's more her type than I am."

"Well, Tyler, I get the feeling this is the first woman you ever loved. I won't say nobody ever died of a broken heart, but you're going to get through this all right. Maybe it will teach you something."

Chapter Twenty-Four

Marybeth liked to get up early, even on Sunday, when the store was closed. It made the weekend longer. After a walk in the cool dampness before dawn, she picked up the paper from the driveway and poured her first cup of coffee. Out on the screened porch, she unfolded the paper.

ENVIRONMENTALIST LINKED TO WILSON TRUST

Professor Gerald Stone, chief architect of the compromise that allowed Wilson Trust to develop their property in the Missitucknee Marsh, is the nephew of Julian Wilson, the founder of the Trust, this paper learned yesterday. According to Mr. Wilson, it was Dr. Stone who suggested, during a visit to New York, that the Trust develop its real estate holdings in Opakulla. "It's the last time I'll listen to Gerald, I assure you," said Mr. Wilson. Development of the property has been halted by the sinkhole that opened in March. The sinkhole has recently grown to encompass virtually all of the Trust land.

Dr. Stone, who is Chairman of the Geology Department at Opakulla University, and long a respected member of Opakulla's environmental community, formed a coalition of environmental groups to forge an agreement with JJ Visions, Inc., developers who represent Wilson Trust. It was largely thanks to his efforts that opponents of the development project withdrew their opposition before the Opakulla Commission in November.

Dr. Stone's mother, who lives in New York, receives a substantial income from the Trust. Jade O'Connell, managing partner of JJ Visions, Inc., expressed surprise at the ties between Dr. Stone and the Wilson Trust. "He was a real tough negotiator, and he got concessions from us that I really didn't want to give. I can't imagine why he never told me about the connection," she said.

Reaction among environmental advocates was mixed. According to Emma Cooper, president of Friends of the Earth and long-time foe of developers, Dr. Stone had betrayed his allies. "I said at the time that the agreement was a betrayal of everything we stand for, and I guess now people will see who the traitor was," she said. But John Raben, of the Sierra Club, urged that people withhold judgment until Dr. Stone has an opportunity to explain his position. "Gerald has been a friend of mine, and a friend of the environment, for over thirty years. I don't believe he would allow his family's financial interests to influence his judgment when it comes to environmental impacts." Dr. Stone could not be reached for comment at his home or office.

Well, this was a treat: a scandal that didn't involve her. Marybeth often dreaded opening the paper. She never knew what she'd find: a distortion of the Commission's actions or her own views, an editorial maligning her. This was an item she could savor with her coffee.

Like all the other Commissioners, she'd voted to permit the development. Now she almost wished she'd voted no, just to make a statement. But with the environmentalists and JJ Visions in such cozy agreement there wasn't any point in opposing it. And she hadn't become a Commissioner to express herself. Her purpose, when she could keep sight of it, was to accomplish something.

Now it looked like Gerald Stone had bamboozled them all. She could be angry, very angry, but with the Trust land so thoroughly swallowed, and the development plans in ruins, there was really no harm done. John Raben was right, too. She shouldn't make any judgments until they'd heard from Dr. Stone. The *Chronicle* had misrepresented her plenty of times. Even when they talked to her, they usually got it wrong.

She ought to talk with Stone herself. She'd only met him once, years ago, at a reception for the new Commissioners, though she'd seen plenty of him during the battle. Really, it was none of her business anymore. No need for the Commission to do anything about the permit, even if they could. The sinkhole had taken care of Sunrise Terrace. She could follow this tempest in a teapot as a spectator. She poured herself another cup of coffee and turned to the gardening section.

—•—

The blackout shade kept the early light from the bedroom window. Helen Stone slipped out of bed without waking Gerald and went into the kitchen for coffee. He had been sleeping so badly, ever since the land disappeared. She was glad to see him sleeping in this morning.

But the closing of the door woke him, and Gerald lay among rumpled sheets examining the last shreds of his dream. He had been giving a speech when he realized everyone in the audience was facing away from him, and the edges of the crowd were unraveling as little knots of people walked away. He kept talking louder, but they just walked faster. They were walking toward something, but now in the half-light coming around the edges of the shade, he had lost the rest of the dream. He was left with a sense of something going on just beyond his view, and he knew Julian was involved.

He hadn't heard anything from Julian since the final sinking of the land. Jade had been in touch with the Trust. He could probably find out something from her.

He was still tired and wished he could go back to sleep, but his mind had woken up. When he lay flat in bed, all the anxious thoughts rose to the surface, so he got up, put on his bathrobe and went into the kitchen.

Helen was measuring coffee into the filter cone when he came in. Her back was toward him, but her stance was peculiar; from their thirty-odd years together he recognized it. She was crying. What on earth could start her crying at the very beginning of the day?

He clamped down on his irritation and spoke gently.

"What is it, darling?"

She turned around and he saw how her face was younger, shined by tears.

"Oh, Gerald, I'm so sorry, there's a terrible article in the paper. It's awful. I wish I could hide it from you."

He looked over at the breakfast nook. She hadn't read the paper, he could see, merely unfolded the front section and then left it there. The headline was all he needed, but of course he read it through to the end.

"If only you could have talked to them first."

"What would I have said? You can't explain something like this."

At least John Raben had stood by him, but would he even be able to explain it to John? Jade O'Connell sounded like she was trying to defend him. But really, Emma was right, it had been a betrayal. How was he going to face people?

Helen brought him a cup of coffee and then sat down across from him in the booth. How many times had they sat in this old-fashioned breakfast nook, remains of breakfast forgotten in front of them, letting the last cups of coffee grow cold, as they talked about anything and everything? Often when they were younger, warmed by their talk, they had gone back to bed from this spot. Late at night too, when he couldn't sleep, he would go quietly into the kitchen to sit in this alcove with a book and a snack. Helen would wake up, and they would have delicious conversations, like children telling secrets.

Now, though, his secret was out, on the front page. Why had he hidden it? Why had he ever taken such an active role in the whole fight? He could have told them that his uncle ran the Trust and therefore he couldn't be involved.

"Darling, you haven't done anything wrong, you know."

"But it looks so bad. They'll never forgive me."

"Your friends will understand, if you explain."

"But what am I going to explain? I told Uncle Julian about the land. Of course now he blames me for the damned sinkhole. And I did everything I could to get the development approved."

"You said yourself, and all the lawyers said, there was no way to prevent it. And right there in the paper, you've got Jade O'Connell, saying you got major concessions from them."

"Great. I've got a developer defending me."

"Look, Gerald. Who are you really worrying about? Most people will forget about this in a week. People like Emma—you can't worry about her. She walks the path of righteousness and is always hoping somebody else will trip. Your real friends, like John, they'll understand."

Gerald was silent for a little while, holding her hand, picking at her cuticle absentmindedly until she drew her hand away.

"I suppose I could write a letter to the *Chronicle*. I just wonder what everyone's thinking right now. Tyler Waites. All the time we've spent together out at the Marsh, and I never said anything to him. And he's always looked up to me."

"Why don't you call him, darling, tell him you want to talk to him. He's such a sensible young man, and he's not a zealot. He's not involved in any of those groups either."

"I'll do that."

She got up to start breakfast, and Gerald turned back to the newspaper. He tried to read something else, but the article drew him back, and he had to read it again. It set off the same hot flush of embarrassment.

"I'd better resign as secretary of the Wilderness Coalition," Helen said quietly, scrambling the eggs with her back turned to him.

"I don't want you to have to do that. You haven't done anything."

"I think it would be best."

She was right, Emma would tear her up in there. If Helen didn't do it herself, someone would probably call for her resignation.

"I have too much to do anyway. I've been wanting to cut back."

Such a transparent lie. They rarely lied to each other. It was extra shame for him. She'd been hoping to be president the following year, and she deserved to be. But there was nothing he could say.

"Do you think it's too early to call Tyler?"

"Why don't you wait till after breakfast."

—•—

Tyler hadn't read the paper. He'd been sitting at his kitchen table, staring at a geology journal, drawing piles of rocks on a yellow pad. He let the phone ring a few times, then decided it might be Carol and leaped up to answer it.

"Oh. Gerald."

"Tyler, I'd like to explain this all to you."

Tyler looked at the phone as if it were an alien artifact.

"Gerald, how did you know about it? Did Carol say something?"

"Carol who? What are you talking about?"

"Carol Willoughby, at the office. Is she upset?"

"Waites, there's some misunderstanding. Have you seen the paper?"

"No."

"I see. Look, are you very busy?"

"No. I'm working on my article for San Francisco, but if there's something you need ...."

"I'd like to meet you for lunch. Somewhere out of town. Why don't we drive down to the café in Missitucknee? I can pick you up. Take a look at the newspaper first, but please, don't make up your mind about anything until you talk to me. "

—•—

Tyler had spent a good part of the morning lying on the couch thinking about Carol. They'd been together such a short time, but it was astonishing how many memories it left him. All of them were bearable except the body memories. Those made him cry. He hadn't cried since he was a child. He'd heard women talk about having a good cry. Carol had told him that she cried at least once a week. Good God. Could she be this miserable? Crying gave him the most horrible, wrenching, helpless feeling, and he stopped as soon as he could.

He would never subject himself to this torment again. Wasn't there some way to have the happiness without all this misery? And would he be able to find his former tranquility, or had Carol stolen that away forever? He was almost angry at her. His life had been perfectly acceptable until she came along.

Tyler was relieved to have something ahead of him, something to take his mind off Carol. Maybe he'd be able to focus on his article until Gerald picked him up. Then he remembered what Gerald had said about the newspaper and went outside to get it.

—•—

Gerald had never been to Tyler's place before. It was a small dark building at the edge of town. The asphalt in the parking lot was uneven, and still held puddles of yesterday's rain. In the wooded area in back was a pile of dirty carpet and a rusted stove.

Tyler's apartment was on the second floor. Gerald climbed the metal stairs. He felt as if he were on a sordid mission in a sordid place. The sky perversely refused to be overcast. It was a sunny, steamy day.

183

He rang the bell and Tyler opened the door. Gerald peered past him into the living room. It had a transient look, though Tyler had lived there over six years. There were no pictures on the walls, and nothing in the living room but a couch, a lamp, a coffee table, and many, many books. He didn't realize that people were still making bookshelves out of cinder blocks and boards. Surely Tyler earned enough to get himself some decent furniture.

Tyler seemed distant. He must have read the newspaper.

"Well, we'd better be going," Tyler said.

"How's your article coming?" Gerald asked

"Pretty good. I expect to have it finished by the end of next week, and I'd like you to read it before I send it off."

"Glad to."

—•—

They were passing the new medical school auditorium, glass and steel set down in the middle of nineteenth century gothic.

"They should have had better sense than to build something like that on the edge of this campus," said Gerald.

"I rather like it. It brightens up the place."

"Oh no, it doesn't fit in at all. You need some sort of unity of design. Helen studied architecture, you know."

Tyler looked at him with interest.

"Never practiced, of course. She never finished college, actually. We got married in her third year of school, and she dropped out."

Tyler said nothing. Gerald focused on his driving. How was he going to get around to the subject? Tyler was quieter than usual, hadn't wanted to talk about his paper. How many times could Gerald be expected to start the conversation? Of course, there was really only one subject that mattered, the reason they were taking this drive, but it was so hard to know how to begin. They were well on their way to Missitucknee, halfway across the Marsh and nearing the Trust land, when Gerald spoke again.

"I suppose you saw the newspaper article."

"Yes."

"Rather embarrassing for me."

"I suppose it is."

"They never talked to me about it you know, they didn't get my side."

"No, that's what it said."

"I'd like to try to explain it to you, see if you can understand."

"Sure."

"Julian Wilson is my mother's older brother. She raised me alone, Tyler, just the two of us, in New York City. It wasn't much of a life for a boy. Not much of a life for her either, I suppose. They lived just two blocks away from us: Julian, Margaret, and their three children. I used to have to go over and play with my cousins every Thursday, and then stay for dinner. A formal dinner, you know, or at least formal compared to anything you see nowadays. Clear soup to start with, cheese after the sweet. The sweet, that's what Margaret called it; she'd spent a year in an English boarding school. Sometimes I think that's why Julian married her. My mother was never invited on Thursdays. I think Julian wanted a chance to work on me without her interfering. We had to go there every Sunday too, the two of us, for dinner after church. Julian was a deacon, of course.

"Julian bullied my mother. He blamed her for marrying my father. My father drank, and he couldn't stand up to Julian. He left us when I was born and Julian would never let my mother mention him. I have some pictures of him though, and the letters he wrote my mother before they were married. I'm named after him. Really, I'm a junior, but I dropped that when I got to college. Julian wanted my mother to change my name after my father left. I was only three months old. I think that was the only time she ever stood up to him. I'd like to have seen it.

"My cousins were two girls and a boy. I didn't have a lot to do with the girls, but Martin was four months older than I was, and we were supposed to be best friends. He was a nice kid really, but we didn't have a lot in common. He didn't do too well in school. It used to make Julian crazy, because I did.

"Martin and I went to the same private school through sixth grade, and then Julian started shifting poor Martin around from place to place, looking for somewhere he could do well enough to get into Harvard. In those days, family meant a lot more and grades meant a lot less, but even so, Martin couldn't get in. It all turned out fine for him. He ended up at the Wharton School of Business and did splendidly. He's the one who runs the Wilson Trust. I don't have anything to do with it, though my mother gets an income from it.

"Well, Julian is pleased as punch with his boy Martin, who really found his niche in business. When I got tenure, Julian made a toast, "Those who can't, teach." He actually said that, like he was joking. My mother looked like he'd slapped her.

"They got the Missitucknee land kind of by accident. They held a bunch of mortgages on a Pennsylvania land speculation outfit that went bankrupt. They didn't even know they had it, or know where Missitucknee was, until I told them. My mother likes me to read the Trust's annual reports for her. She's never said so, but I sometimes think she doesn't quite trust Martin, and Julian has convinced her that she can't understand financial affairs. So I read them, and about ten years ago, I saw they had acquired the Marsh property. The paper got it right. I did suggest that they develop it.

"I can't explain it to you, Tyler. We were all sitting around after Thanksgiving dinner a few years ago—God how I hate those Thanksgivings, but Helen likes them, and my mother wouldn't understand if I didn't go. They were talking about wanting to do some property development, something to do with the market and taxes, and I just popped out with it. I would have given anything to take it back. When there started being all this trouble for them, Julian expected me to fix it, and of course, you know, nobody was going to be able to stop the development exactly, just slow it down and complicate it. Julian and Martin had started to take it personally, and Julian swore to me that he didn't care whether they made a profit. He was even willing to lose money; it was the principle of the thing. So I had to get involved, because I knew he meant what he said, and I figured I had to try to protect the Marsh as much as possible."

Gerald had never looked at Tyler all the time he was talking but kept his eyes on the road. Still, somehow he had failed to notice the turn-off to Missitucknee.

"My God, I've driven clear past it. Why didn't you say something?"

"I didn't want to interrupt you."

"Are you hungry?"

"No."

"Neither am I. What do you say we just turn around at Lowilla and drive home? We can get a hamburger in town if you like. I really didn't care about lunch. I just wanted to explain all this to you."

Tyler was touched. And while Gerald had been talking, he had half-forgotten about Carol. He was grateful to have something else to think about.

The newspaper article had struck him as rather slimy. It didn't tell anything about the issues that had been involved in the development of the property. Tyler took a dim view of newspapers. He had on several occasions given careful explanations to a reporter only to see a mostly garbled account in the paper the next day. He could picture the publisher smiling with delight over a new scandal. It would sell extra copies for at least a week if they played their cards right and stretched it out.

"Helen and I are going to have to resign from the Friends of the Marsh after this."

"Oh no, Gerald. People will understand."

"Most people won't want to understand, Tyler. And how would I explain to them? I may lose a lot of my friends over this. The *Chronicle* isn't going to publish an account of my childhood. It's really not an explanation anyway; I don't know why I told you all that. You know, somehow you feel like family to me. Helen feels the same way. That's why it was important to me that you understand."

Chapter Twenty-Five

Carol had a plot in the community garden over on the east side of town. She liked to get out there early, before the sun got too hot, but this morning Christopher and Robin had started squabbling over the trowel. Their grandmother had given each of them a set of gardening tools for Christmas; now they could only find one of the trowels, and Carol didn't know whose it was.

"I had the blue one, Mommy, don't you remember?"

"You did not, I got the blue one because I'm the boy, dummy."

"Christopher, that's enough, you know we don't call names. You two can share the blue one, or we can just leave it home and you can dig with your forks."

"Well, I don't even want to go to the stupid garden," Robin said.

"I don't want to hear another peep out of you. Go get dressed."

Now Robin was sitting on her bed, wearing nothing but her underpants. Carol could see her through the half-opened door. She had taken the shoelaces out of her sneakers and was trying different ways of lacing them. The curve of her little back spoke volumes, but Carol was in no mood to listen. Christopher was out in the backyard tormenting the dog. She poured herself a glass of tea and picked up a magazine.

When she'd finished the tea she called, "Robin, NOW."

After a thud and several banging drawers, Robin appeared, looking triumphant. She wore her best party dress. Carol considered saying something, but she just didn't have the strength.

"Get your basket and fork, and let's go."

—•—

Carol had neglected the plot for several weeks. They'd had lots of rain, and the weeds were flourishing. Still, the tomatoes and marigolds looked healthy. Under the weeds she found a single zucchini that she'd somehow missed on her last visit. It had grown to twice its previous size. She wondered if you could eat something that large. Maybe she should let the kids carve it like a pumpkin. The melon vines were luxuriant but there was no sign of fruit. Two plots over, the melons were as big as bowling balls. She'd never had any luck with melons.

Christopher had settled down in his corner to weed. This was the one place where she could count on him to behave himself. He was a born gardener. Robin stood in her corner looking dainty. She was afraid to get her dress dirty. Carol sent her over to the playground to swing in the shade.

"Next time, honey, you might want to wear shorts."

It was close to eleven by the time Carol got to work. She was planning to pull up the last of the zucchini and put in some zinnias. The sets looked a bit unhappy. She'd had them for three weeks, and their stringy little roots were bursting out of the drain holes. They were wilting fast in the heat, but she thought if she fussed over them enough, they might make it.

Carol never had much success with the garden. Either she would wait too long to plant, or she'd count on rain when there wasn't any, or she'd forget the plot for a few weeks and come back to find that the weeds had won. But every time she planted, her enthusiasm sprouted up again. She loved the smell of the dirt, the hot sun on her back, digging in, and getting her fingernails grimy. She loved the peace between the children. They never quarreled at the garden.

The plot right next to hers was cultivated by an Indian woman, Madhuri. She was a skilled gardener, and always happy to give advice. She raised eleven kinds of peppers—most of them from seeds her mother sent from India. Madhuri was quiet and shy, and Carol found it easy to talk with her.

As a girl, and in college, Carol had always had a best friend, but after she got married and dropped out of school, she didn't have anyone to talk to but her husband, and Jack didn't think she needed to talk to anyone else. When the children were babies, she would sit in the lush playground in Miami and listen to the rapid Spanish of the other mothers. Sometimes when one of them was alone, she would try to strike up a conversation, but their answers were only polite.

When she left Jack, moved to Opakulla, and found a job, she thought that she would finally have friends again. Now it seemed as if she had lost the habit of friendship. The other secretaries invited her along to lunch when the whole group was going, but nobody ever asked her to go out just the two of them. And when she was with the group, she never had anything to say. She could tell a story about Christopher, but they seemed to stop listening when she was halfway through.

She could do without a lover a whole lot easier than she could do without a friend, yet she always had some man sniffing around, and she couldn't make friends anymore. She was like those girls in high school who never fit in. They bought all the right clothes, but the clothes hung funny. They used all the right slang, but they sounded like grown-ups pretending to be teenagers. The other girls avoided them as if they were contagious. They tried and tried and had it all wrong.

She liked talking to Madhuri, who assumed Carol had it all right. Madhuri seemed to be as lonely as she was and welcomed her talk in the garden. Still, it had never gone beyond the garden. She had asked if they could get together for lunch during the week, but Madhuri said, "No, I am very busy all of the time," with a brilliant smile, as if she were accepting an award. Their conversation in the garden never got beyond the children, and the fact that Madhuri's husband was a graduate student in horticulture. Carol was embarrassed to ask her about her life in India. She felt she ought to know about it already. Or maybe Madhuri would be offended if Carol noticed that she was a foreigner.

Carol worked for over an hour. Christopher had joined Robin at the swings, and miraculously, they were taking turns pushing each other. She had pulled up all the zucchini vines, and the melon vines too, and set in the zinnias. They looked a little sorry, drooping as they did. She hadn't bought enough to fill the space, but she could bring more next week. Maybe she would buy some different colors.

She noticed Madhuri looking past her and turned around. Someone had parked a big silver BMW at the edge of the dusty parking lot and was walking toward them. It took her only a moment to recognize Randall.

"I saw your car, and the children in the playground, and thought I'd stop and say hello."

She stood up, brushing the dirt off her knees. She knew she looked a mess. Her hair stuck to her face with sweat, and she got all red and mottled in heat like this.

"You look like you could use a drink."

"I have some iced tea in the car."

"Would you like me to get it for you?"

"Sure."

She joined him on the bench in the playground. There were three plastic glasses, so she gave one to each of the kids, and she and Randall shared.

"Why are you here?"

That was Christopher. He was digging with a stick, throwing little clods of dirt up next to Randall's foot.

"I was just driving by and saw you all in the garden, and I thought I'd stop and say hello to your mother."

"Are you going to eat lunch with us? We only have three sandwiches."

Carol didn't like Christopher to be rude, and she thought of intervening, but decided to let Randall rescue himself. These battles were better fought by the principals.

"If you'd like, I can take you all out to lunch."

"Oh, yay! Can we go Mommy?" Robin had always liked Randall. When he was around she acted extra cute and ladylike, a real Miss Priss.

"Can we go to Burgerland?" asked Christopher.

"If it's all right with your mother."

It was all right with her, she supposed. It was undeniable: that first, unexpected sight of Randall had sent a shiver through her. But lunch with him couldn't get her in any trouble, not with the kids, not at Burgerland.

—•—

193

Randall was impressive at Burgerland. He merely averted his eyes when Christopher blew his straw wrapper across the room. Even when Robin spilled her milkshake, and it splattered his shirt, he took it calmly, though Carol thought his knuckles looked a little white as he blotted it up. He offered to buy another milkshake for Robin, and told her not to worry, it would all come out in the wash. In between orders, and spills, and eating, he managed to tell Carol that he was planning to buy a house.

"I guess you had to give up the idea of Sunrise Terrace, huh?"

"Yes. They won't be building there for a long time. They say there won't be much delay in getting my deposit back."

"You'll need it if you're looking for a house. How come you're not looking at another condo?"

"There weren't any others in town that suited me. Sunrise Terrace was the only one I've seen that I'd be willing to live in. And I think I'd enjoy having my own house. I might want to do some gardening."

"Where are you looking?"

"Well, tomorrow I'm looking at two places in Hidden Pond and one in Valley Ridge."

"God, Randall, you're talking bucks!"

She didn't miss his slightly pained look, though he covered it quickly. Same old Randall.

"Listen. Do you think you might come with me? It would really help to have a second opinion. The agent is good, but of course she's looking for a commission. I'd like to know what you think."

"Oh, I don't know. What would I do with the kids? Can you see them tearing through those houses?"

"You can get a babysitter, can't you?"

"That's expensive."

"I'll pay for it. After all, you'd be doing me a favor."

This was something new.

—•—

They met the realtor at her office. She was Carol's age, but from a different planet. Her suit was real silk, her jewelry real gold, her car a real Mercedes, and her husband a real doctor.

They drove to the very edge of town. The road wound in through an ancient oak hammock. The builders had left some of the larger trees, so it was cool and shady. The houses were set back at the end of long curving drives, with miniature houses sheltering the mailboxes. They blended together in Carol's mind: parquet floors, cathedral ceilings, screened pools, and dizzying numbers of closets.

In one, Randall asked Carol, "Do you like the kitchen? It would be wonderful for parties, wouldn't it?"

"You don't give parties."

"Well, I haven't, but that's because I don't have any place for them. I'm looking for a home now."

In another, he asked the realtor, "What kind of neighborhood is this? Is it mostly retired people? I don't see any children."

"No, you'll find it's very quiet. This is mostly singles and retired couples. Families tend to go to other neighborhoods."

In the third, the realtor asked Carol, "When is the wedding?"

"The wedding? Oh, no, we're not getting married. I just came along for advice. We're old friends."

—•—

After they left the realtor back at her office, they went to Romano's for a drink on the shaded patio. Carol was silent until the waiter left. She watched Randall. He was the best-looking man she had ever known, big-boned with fine skin and brown velvet eyes. Just looking at his face she could feel it under her fingers.

"So what did you think?" he asked.

"I think she thinks you're gay."

"I think you're right."

"Does it bother you?"

"Not really. Oh, a little I suppose."

"Is that why you brought me along?"

"No!"

He sounded truly shocked. She knew perfectly well why he had brought her along. Randall was so obvious. She couldn't understand why he wanted to get back together. Of course, she was the one who had broken it off. But that was months ago; she hadn't heard from him in a long time. There was so much about her that bothered him. Why didn't he go find someone suitable, some rich bitch, like that realtor Jeanne what's-her-name? But he was acting different now—he seemed to be trying to please her, not merely tolerating her. How long could this last? Could they possibly get back together and make it work?

Obviously, he was shopping for a house for the two of them. A little presumptuous, she thought. The question was, did she want him back? She knew she did. If she could have back the passion, the understanding, if he could bring her into his world without apologizing for her. If she and Randall could make it together, maybe she could quit her job, go back to school. But she had to be careful. Had he really changed, or was this just courtship behavior?

"Carol, how could you…I thought…don't you think maybe we should try again, the two of us together I mean? I didn't think I would, but I miss you terribly. I'd really like to try. We could make it different this time."

"Oh, Randall, I don't know."

"You think I don't give you credit for what you've done. But I do admire you, really. This time I'd make an effort with the kids. There was something special between us. You know I still turn you on."

And just the way he said it, the assurance that entered his voice, the way he looked at her, that was a turn on in itself, she had to admit. Couldn't she just go to bed with him again? She wouldn't be committing herself to anything. But no, then she would slide right back into the same old shit. The only way was to take it slow, keep the upper hand for a while. If he wanted her back, he could damn well make an effort. She'd give him some time and see if things really could be different.

Chapter Twenty-Six

At JJ Visions Inc., the phone wouldn't stop ringing. Jasmine was frantic. Leland Forrest, Laneer Sand and Gravel, everybody was calling to find out when they were going to get paid. Some of them hadn't even sent bills yet, but with the project in ruins, they wanted to make sure their money didn't disappear down the sinkhole.

It would be up to the Trust to pay the bills. But Jade was the one who dealt with the people at the Trust, and she didn't have a clue where Jade was. Early that morning while she was in the bathroom, she'd heard the front door close. In the kitchen the newspaper was on the table, and not a sign of Jade. It wasn't like her, to take off like this without a word.

—•—

Jade had gone to the Marsh. In hiking boots and shorts, she scrambled down the steep slope. She leaned forward and let her feet catch up with her body in great leaps. She leaned back and jolted down, digging in with her heels. She lost her footing and went slipping and sliding on her rump, and finally she reached the bottom.

First, a long drink from her canteen. Down so deep, there ought to be a pond, or at least a puddle to cool off in. She bent over and touched the dirt. It was damp in spots. But it was hot everywhere. The sun poured down mercilessly into the great open bowl. She turned slowly, following the rim of the sink with her eyes. Not a hawk nor a cloud crossed the great blue sky, pale in the heat. The steep, sloping sides were nothing but dust and fallen trees, and the small skeletons of fish on the ground had been picked dry.

She walked over to a fallen oak and found a broken patch of shade. She took off her shirt, wet it from the canteen, and wiped off her face. Then she leaned back against a root, closed her eyes, and let the magic of the Marsh take over.

They wouldn't be building any Sunrise Terrace. No beautiful office park either. *I would have built good ones, too,* said a child's voice inside. "Yeah, you would have," she said out loud. She stretched her neck to press the root into her shoulders and a tear slid down into her ear.

Pictures flashed through her mind. Meetings in New York, sitting around that long walnut table. Sunrise Terrace, vivid as if they had built it, the early sun flashing off the windows, the buildings barely visible behind the giant oaks. One of those oaks sheltered her now. Peering through the roots along the great trunk, she could see the scrap of yellow plastic hanging limp.

She and Jasmine had gone to the site to watch on the day the bulldozers began their slow crawl, squat and stubborn, shoving down the trees. When the first tree fell, she grabbed Jasmine's hand and squeezed. She could feel that hand in hers now, thin in the fingers, strong in the palm, a guitar-playing hand.

Jasmine at fourteen, singing folk songs, her hair down over her shoulders in coppery ripples. Jasmine's hair wasn't quite so bright now, but it was still soft. They used to take turns brushing each other's hair. They hadn't done that in a long time. Her own hair was straightened and cut short now. She picked up a pebble and began rolling it in her fingers. It was a fossil, a tiny piece of an ancient peccary, but she had no way of knowing that. Some thought was trying to push up out of the shambles in her head. She didn't want to spend the rest of her life reading regulations and filling out forms, meeting and haggling and arguing. She didn't want to put her dreams out there in the world for people to fill with their furniture, their children, their lives. No homes, no office plazas, no buildings up to the sky. Suddenly that urge was gone, as sure as the land was gone, swallowed up by this great and lovely hole. And she didn't want to spend another minute pretending to be what she wasn't. Those years together with Jasmine when they were young and traveling free—those were the best years.

Carrying her shirt and canteen, she scrambled out from under the roots. She stood up, hoping for a breeze, but the air barely moved. At her feet, when she looked close, green sprouts were poking through the dirt. Probably sandspurs, she thought. Still, these tiny signs of life were cheering. And now she saw others. A lizard peered at her from behind a clump of dirt, motionless except for his throbbing red throat. A line of fire ants advanced to their mound. She put on her shirt and began the long hot climb up out of the hole.

—•—

She drove straight to the office and found a message from Gerald, but Jasmine was gone. She called home and got no answer. Jasmine hadn't even left the machine on—the phone rang and rang—so she called Gerald and agreed to meet him for a drink. A lot of the bars near campus closed when the students were gone, but the Blue Frog stayed open all summer. It was dark and quiet, almost empty.

200

—•—

Gerald had told Jade everything, and now he was waiting for her to say something. But she just sat there, looking down at her beer, rubbing her finger back and forth in the circle of water on the table. There was something different about her, and he couldn't figure out what it was.

It wasn't just the way she was dressed. He'd seen her in hiking clothes before, though he'd never seen her quite like this; smudged, scratched, and thoroughly disheveled. And she wasn't responding to what he was telling her. There was a distance of some kind; he couldn't put his finger on it. He had always felt so close to her.

"You know, Jade, you may be the only friend I have left in this town."

What an odd look she gave him then. She seemed almost angry. What did she have to be angry about?

"Gerald, I hope for your sake that's not true. Jasmine and I don't have anything holding us here anymore. We're leaving."

Well, of course, he should have thought of that. The sinkhole had destroyed everything she'd been working on. No wonder she was upset.

"That's terrible! I hate to see you go. Listen, I hope you understand about my family, I mean, why I never told you."

"We all have our secrets, Gerald."

She picked up her glass of beer and swallowed what was left.

"I have to be going. I have a lot to do."

She was gone before he could really talk to her. He had been so sure she would understand and stick by him.

—•—

"Jasmine, I'm back."

Jade was calling even before she was through the front door. No answer. She called again, and Jasmine came down the hall.

"Dammit, I heard you the first time. I was trying to take a nap."

"Oh, Jas, I'm sorry."

"I should think so. Where the hell have you been?"

"Deep down the rabbit hole and back, and now, listen to where we're going."

"You've been off getting stoned, and I've been working my ass off? The phone just never quit, and I finally had to turn off the ringer, all those people wanting to talk to you. For chrissake Jade, what's gotten into you?"

Because Jade was just standing there, smiling at her.

"I'm back," she said softly.

Chapter Twenty-Seven

Tyler was sitting on the edge of his bed, staring out the back window into the woods. His hands were poised on the mattress, ready to push him up, but all the force seemed to have drained from his muscles. He had already gotten up once this morning, resolutely dressed and breakfasted. He was standing with an armful of dirty clothes, reaching for one last sock, when suddenly pointlessness rose up in front of him like a flat gray wall, causing him to sink down on the side of the bed and sit. Without his willing it, his mind named the trees outside, noted the mockingbird, not yet singing. A blue jay flew off and returned to the same branch again. The power had gone off briefly in the night, and the clock repeatedly flashed 12:00.

Carol's absence was a constant presence. It greeted him in the morning and lurked in the background all day. It only left at night when, if he dreamed of her, he dreamed they were together again.

Silently he repeated the list of Saturday chores, which he'd made so carefully the night before, hoping to avoid this state, but it was a chant that bore no relation to his actually standing up and beginning the day. He was stuck in neutral.

The phone delivered him. It was Carol. Hope battled heartbreak, and Tyler being Tyler, hope won.

"How are you?"

"Oh, I'm fine, I mean I'm okay. But Tyler, I need to talk to you; it's about the dog."

"The dog?"

His thoughts had been miles from any dog, and he struggled to remember.

"Yes, Duster, the puppy you gave us."

"What about her?"

"Tyler, she's just too much for me to handle. She's chewing everything, and I can't get her housebroken. I don't have time to train her, and she's driving me crazy. You'll have to take her back."

"I can't take her back to the pound. They'd have to put her to sleep."

"Well, maybe someone else will adopt her. Or maybe you could keep her yourself. She's good company, and you'd have more time for her than I do."

It wasn't what he'd hoped, but maybe this was her way of saying she wanted to see him again, or maybe when they were together she would change her mind. He promised to come over that afternoon.

He picked up the laundry from where he had let it drop and stuffed it in the bag. Sometimes he sat downstairs with the newspaper while the machine ran through its cycle, but now he had too much to do. He didn't want to arrive at Carol's empty-handed.

—•—

Tyler hadn't been in a toy store since he was a child. And he'd never been in a toy store like this one. Outside, shopping carts were lined up, more than he'd ever seen in a grocery store. Who used a shopping cart to buy toys? When he was little, you bought them one at a time.

Inside, the store was as big as a warehouse. In the first aisle, he came to the water pistols, but not just pistols. Water jets, the Exterminator, Wet Action Tanks, Laser spray guns. Some of them would hold a quart of water. Briefly, Tyler considered one each for Christopher and Robin. Maybe for him and Carol too. But the picture of pandemonium that rose before him gave him pause.

Down past the dolls were the pastel ponies, with deformed faces and heads you could twist to make their tails grow. He knew about these—Robin had several. But he couldn't bring himself to buy her another.

She'd showed them to him the first time he ate dinner at their house. Robin and Christopher shared a room, but the difference in the two sides was as good as a wall. On Chris's side, it was Spiderman everywhere, including the sheets. The floor was covered with little creatures: ninja turtles, transformers, round wooden people with flat heads and smiling faces, dozens of small plastic dinosaurs. A soldier doll with jungle gear. Tyler had called it a doll just once. "It's not a doll. It's a action figure." And Chris raised the doll's arm with the M-16 in it and pointed it at Tyler. Tyler was a little taken aback.

Robin's side was less cluttered. Half her toys were in baskets rather than on the floor. Her sheets were yellow with white eyelet ruffles. The ponies were lined up on the bookcase.

"They're kind of babyish, don't you think?" She looked at him anxiously.

"Oh, I don't know. Not if you like them."

She reached out to fix the chartreuse pony's tail.

Wandering up and down the aisles of the store, Tyler was losing interest in toys. Did that happen to children when they came in here? Twenty-four aisles ran front to back, and four across. There was a whole wall lined from floor to ceiling with games. Maybe he could find something there. But he wanted to get them each a separate present. He felt blinded by all the bright plastic. He'd given up and was leaving, when he saw the soap bubbles at the checkout counter. Gratefully he bought two bottles and escaped. He stopped by the florist on the way to Carol's.

Christopher was on the front porch when he arrived. It had only been a few weeks since he'd seen him, but Tyler felt he had been away forever.

"Hello, Christopher."

"Here, can you make this track stay together? It keeps coming out."

It was a plastic racing car track. It did indeed keep coming out. The coupling didn't fit. Korean women in white masks, stamping out millions of bright plastic pieces. Or was it only the Chinese who wore masks? Maybe one section of track had been made in Korea and the other in China, and that's why they didn't fit together.

"I hate this old track. I told my Mom what to get but she never gets the right kind."

"Maybe we can go to the store together and you can show me what you need. Here, I brought you something."

He handed him the bubbles.

"Neat. Can we go to the store now?"

"No, I need to talk to your mother. Is she upstairs?"

"Yeah. Hey, are you going to take Duster away?"

"I think so."

"No fair. You gave her to us."

"Well, Chris, your Mom says Duster's too much trouble."

"I can take care of her. I feed her and everything. She just doesn't like it cause Duster chewed the rug."

Tyler felt helpless. Christopher stood in front of the screen door like a small sentinel, only his face was starting to crumple up.

"Maybe you can come play with Duster at my house. You could help me give her a bath. And maybe when she's bigger and learns how to behave she can live with you again."

He was dangerously close to saying they could all live together. He opened the door and started upstairs. Behind him he could hear Christopher kicking on the screen.

Carol opened the door at the top of the stairs. She was wearing shorts and a faded red halter top. Tyler thrust the flowers forward.

"Tyler, you shouldn't have."

She looked concerned.

"Hey, it's not diamonds. The bubbles are for Robin. I gave Christopher his present downstairs."

"Here you are doing me a favor, and you're bringing us presents. I've got Duster in the backyard. Can I get you some tea or something? I better put these in water."

She hurried away from him into the kitchen. Of course, she was bound to feel awkward until they got things resolved.

"It's so good to see you. I've missed you," Tyler said.

She kept her back turned, running water into a jar, getting out the pitcher of iced tea and two glasses. Tyler sat on the couch. She came in the living room and put the tea in front of him on the table, then moved the newspaper out of the armchair and sat down.

"I was telling Christopher maybe he can come play with Duster sometimes."

"Oh Tyler, I don't think so. It would be confusing to him to go on seeing you."

"Confusing how?"

"Well, I've been seeing Randall again. You know Randall, that I told you about."

She didn't want him back. He'd really known it when she opened the door.

"But you said...."

"I know what I said, but things are different between us now. Randall is different. He's really trying. I think it did us good to split up for a while. He seems to appreciate me more. Remember how I told you I thought he was ashamed of me? Well, he's taking me to the Governor's wedding next month in Tallahassee. He's paying for the babysitter, and he even offered to buy me a new dress. But I told him no. See, I don't want to get too involved too fast. If we get married, it's going to be on my terms."

"You're thinking of getting married."

"He hasn't said anything. But he's shopping for a house, and he says things like, "It would be nice for the kids to have a pool." And that's another thing. He's different with the kids. Robin always liked him a lot, but Christopher used to be really awful when he was around. I told you about the time he squirted like a quart of ketchup on Randall's french fries. So Randall is giving Chris a lot of attention now. He told him he'd take him to the studio and show him how to work the equipment. And he's talking about taking them both to Disney World. They'd love that. They've never been, and I've always wanted to take them, but I couldn't afford it."

He should have taken them to Disney World.

"You know, Tyler, if I married Randall, I could change my whole life. I could finish college. I wouldn't have to struggle anymore."

"I would have married you."

"Oh, Tyler. You and me, it just wasn't there for us. We're too different. You're wonderful as a friend…."

"I see."

"Oh. I guess you don't really want to talk about Randall."

"No. Maybe you'd better get Duster's things together."

How stupid he was. If she'd wanted to get back together, she would have said so on the phone. He put Robin's bubbles on the table next to the flowers, stuck in the little jar any which way.

—•—

Duster bounced out of the backyard and squirmed all the way to the car, but when he drove with one hand rubbing her ears she lay quiet on the passenger seat. There was comfort in her soft fur. She just needed attention. Like Christopher. Could Duster be bought with trips to Disney World? He hadn't needed to buy Chris; they were friends without it. Or Carol, for that matter. Of course, he didn't have Carol.

It bothered him that he hadn't had a last time with her, knowing it was the last time. He should have grabbed her when she came to the door, all that warm flesh exposed, buried his face in her skin, had one more armful of her. Now it was too late. Friends. Sure, they could be friends. She could talk to him for hours about Randall. Maybe he could help her plan her strategy. Hell, he could help her plan the wedding.

Duster licked his hand. His one souvenir. He'd been with Carol less than three months. She'd walked in, totally disrupted his life, and then walked out, leaving him with Duster. When they were together, small delights took him by surprise. Now memories lay in ambush. One night Carol had laughed in her sleep, clear and musical. How could he go on without the possibility of that bright ribbon of laughter suddenly floating beside him in the night? He would become a grumpy old man with a dog.

Chapter Twenty-Eight

The So Long Summer picnic in Memorial Park was the biggest celebration in Opakulla. Munro had volunteered to wear the clown costume and sit in the dunking booth. Marybeth had stayed with him awhile, sitting at the ticket table next to Larry Hogue, who was playing carnival barker. She didn't like to watch Munro in the dunking chair, clowning and fooling, calling out to his friends in the crowd, and then the look of helpless surprise when the ball hit the target and he felt the chair fall out from under him. Showing off, she called it. It had been cute when he was sixteen.

She pulled her purse out from under the table and wandered off to see what there was to see. She stopped at the Rotary booth for a hotdog and lemonade. From somewhere they had gotten a giant hotdog cooker. The hotdogs were impaled on hot spikes, raw-looking.

"Marybeth, let me give you a wiener." It was Cleland Dewar, president of the board of realtors, smiling and sweating and holding out a swollen pink sausage. "No, you put your money away. I guess we can afford to treat a Commissioner once in a while."

"Now, Cleland, you wouldn't want somebody to think I was taking bribes." She smiled right back at him and laid her dollar on the table. Covered with mustard, the hotdog tasted ok. In less than a year, she wouldn't have to smile at Cleland Dewar unless he was buying nails. And he wouldn't care anymore if she did.

She carried her hotdog over to where the Boy Scouts were running an egg toss. Marybeth kept her eye on one little girl in a ruffled pink dress. All the other kids were wearing shorts and sneakers, but this little girl looked like she'd been dressed for a wedding. She held her hands up together, making a little basket, and unerringly caught the egg, time after time. And each time, she sent it back with a fierce overhand throw, straight to her opponent. She'd retired two boys already—one got the egg on his elbow, and one on the chin. Marybeth couldn't leave until it was over.

They were down to just three kids when the little girl finally fumbled, and the egg, a hard throw, hit her in the chest. She stood stock still a moment, and then looked down and saw the yellow slime dripping down her front. She opened her mouth wide and let out a loud wail, and into the ring rushed her mother, in a sundress and white sandals, with glossy pink toenails.

"Now Tara Lynn, I TOLD you you didn't want to be throwing eggs with your party dress on, but you wouldn't listen to me."

Marybeth had never seen them before. When she was growing up, she would have known everyone at the picnic. And that little girl would never have been throwing eggs if her mama told her no.

She wandered on past the 4-H booth. Now that there wasn't a county fair anymore, they had their cooking contest at the picnic. She had never been much of a cook, but she did know about preserves, and before she got on the Commission, she used to enter her blueberry jam. One year she'd won a red ribbon. She didn't have time anymore for making jam. She and Munro still picked the berries off the bushes they'd planted in the backyard, but now what they couldn't eat right away she just put up in the freezer. This year the blue ribbon went to a jar of spiced peach preserves. She looked at the nametag. Sarita Echevarria.

Three elementary schools had put on an art display. Lots of smiling stick figures with great yellow suns above them. Horses with broomstraw tails.

Off at the far end of the park, by the picnic tables, the Future Farmers of America had set up a petting zoo, really a petting farm, with baby goats, piglets, and one gangly calf. Two women were leaning on the fence. They each had one foot up on the rail, their bottoms sticking out, one big bottom in faded jeans, one smaller bottom in loose white shorts. Marybeth stared at their red hair and realized it was Jade O'Connell and her twin sister, whom she'd never met. She walked over and leaned on the fence next to them.

"Hello, Jade."

"Marybeth, how nice to see you. This is my sister, Jasmine. Jas, this is Marybeth Coggins, from the Commission. I've told you about her."

Marybeth was always interested by people's families. She liked to match up their faces and see how the same expressions ran through them. Twins were good. These two looked a lot alike, but Jade looked older. It was mostly the hair, she decided. Jade's hair was cut short and tidy; Jasmine's fell over her shoulders in a great rippling bush. But the color was the same, more carrot than brick. She'd never seen Jade in jeans, and they made her look different. She seemed bigger, stronger, and more relaxed. She was certainly friendlier. All the reserve was gone.

"I'm glad to run into you here, Marybeth. I wouldn't want to leave town without saying goodbye to you."

Jade and her sister were giving up their business and going traveling. They were just going to pile their things in a van and go wherever they wanted. Marybeth had thought of doing the same thing with Munro when they retired. She knew people who traveled half the year in their Winnebagos. Of course, she didn't know how she and Munro would ever get a chance to retire. Who would mind the store? Jade wasn't anywhere near retirement age, though. She couldn't be much more than forty. It seemed a shame to give it all up and wander around like a couple of hippies just when their company was beginning to grow.

"Sunrise Terrace must have been a real disappointment, I know. But other projects will come along. People speak real well of you. I think your business is ready to pick up."

"I'm tired of business, Marybeth. Look at me. Look at us. We don't fit in with those guys. All their deals and smiles and slaps on the back. We had big dreams, but I didn't know what it would be like. Maybe when dreams come true you get a lot of stuff you don't expect. I love building, but I can't stand the rest. I don't know how you do it on the Commission. I never thought you really fit in there either."

"It's different growing up here, Jade. I've known these people all my life."

"You know, it's funny. I never could figure out where you were coming from on Sunrise Terrace. You own a business. I would have thought you'd want to encourage development."

"I do, I guess. I took a lot of heat for it, you know. But the Marsh is special. It seems like outsiders want to come buy up all our special places, keep them all for themselves. And then they ruin them. No offense, I'm sure you would have done a real nice job. But the Marsh—you can't go building houses on the Marsh."

"We sure can't now." That was Jasmine. She had a funny, gravelly voice. "Have you seen that sinkhole?"

"I went out there back in May. I haven't seen it since it stopped growing."

The whole Commission had gone together, accompanied by a *Chronicle* reporter. It was funny to see them all in their outdoor clothes. They trailed dutifully behind Eugene Caruthers, the director of public safety. Ken and Delmar started clowning around, throwing clods of dirt, challenging each other to race down to the bottom. It was like being on a school field trip.

Eugene was a picture, trying to tell his bosses to behave themselves. "The terrain still isn't stable. There's a danger of slides."

Randall had worn new hiking boots, and he was limping by the time they'd walked all the way around. He looked bored and uncomfortable, and he was having the most trouble with the mosquitoes; he had on short pants. She gave him some of her repellant. The *Chronicle* reported it the next day and left out all the good stuff. They made it sound dull as a budget workshop. She'd like to go back sometime, just by herself or maybe with Munro, and explore it. Not till October though, when the weather cooled down a little.

"It would be neat if someone had filmed it over a few months, so we could see it happen," said Jasmine. "When we've seen the U.S., we might go on around the world, looking for sinkholes and canyons. We could follow the fault lines and look for earthquakes."

"No earthquakes, Jas. I wouldn't want to lose you."

And Jade looked at her with the most tender expression, squeezed her hand. It was nice to see sisters so close.

"Well, Jade, I'm real glad to have seen you before you go. If you come back through Opakulla anytime, you be sure to come by the store, let me know how you're doing. Jasmine, it was nice to meet you. I hope you have a good trip."

The heat was becoming unbearable. The music was starting over at the band shell. It would be restful to sit and listen to the band, watch the people go by. She wondered if it was worth the trouble to go get her lawn chair. The car was parked a block away, but she wasn't going to be able to sit on the ground for very long, and it would be hours before Munro finished over at the dunking booth.

On the way back from the car she bought herself a large glass of iced tea. She found a place in the shade, set up her chair, and settled in. She liked this, sitting cool and quiet with her own thoughts, listening and not listening to the music.

Now they had the Orange River Barbershop Singers up there. There were eight of them, and a very odd assortment they were. One of the tenors was a fat pink man with a shiny bald head and thick glasses. His partner was long and bony. His hair was in a limp ponytail, and he wore a single earring. One baritone was a square-jawed, short-haired blonde boy, looked like one of those Mormon missionaries she'd seen riding around on bicycles. And there was a big muscular guy, with tattoos all over his forearms. How had they ever gotten together, and what on earth did they talk about when they weren't singing?

She'd chosen her spot out of the main line of traffic, but still every few minutes somebody would walk by, say, "Hey there, Commissioner," give a wave. She smiled and waved at every one of them, though it made her nervous that she didn't know their names.

She never could remember names. It was amazing that she'd ever been elected. She'd sent away for a mail order course once, early in her term, hoping it could help her at the endless meetings and receptions. People got a little tight around the eyes the fourth time she was introduced to them. The course advised her to associate every name with something unusual about the person. So if she met someone with a dimple in his chin, and his name was Holthouse, she was supposed to think "dimple, hole, holthouse" when she saw him again. But she was just as likely to call the guy Mr. Chin. And at receptions she was meeting two people a minute. If she tried to find a key in everybody's face, she couldn't listen to what they were saying to her. Maybe it would have worked if she'd actually taken classes and had a chance to practice it.

"Hello, Marybeth."

It was Randall. No trouble recognizing him. But the woman with him, with two children, was a stranger. Randall was loaded down, with two lawn chairs in each hand. The woman carried a picnic basket. She had a nice face, with sandy hair a little straggly in the heat.

"I'd like you to meet Carol Willoughby. And these are her children, Robin and Christopher. Do you mind if we join you?"

Of course she minded. But she couldn't think quickly of any nice way to say no. Why on earth Randall would want to sit with her, she couldn't imagine. Though the lawn chairs must be getting awfully heavy, and the shady spots were filling up fast.

It was always interesting watching Randall, when he didn't make her so mad she lost her sense of humor. And it would certainly be interesting to see what kind of woman he'd hooked up with. She would have pictured Randall with someone very different. Someone thin and elegant. Maybe someone younger. Certainly not this slightly plump, pleasant-faced woman. And certainly not someone with children.

The children were fussing. Carol was setting out their picnic, but they wanted hotdogs from the vendor.

"Oh, it's all right Carol, let them eat what they want. Here, Robin, here's five dollars."

Marybeth didn't miss Carol's slight frown. It looked like she was about to say something to Randall, but instead she turned to Marybeth,

"Would you like a sandwich? I have peanut butter and jelly, or cream cheese and raisins."

"Why don't you offer her some of the good food? We picked up salads and cheese at Mario's."

"Actually, peanut butter and jelly will do me fine. I don't have it very often since my kids left home."

Carol asked about her children, where they were, what they were doing. Randall shifted his chair so that it was angled just the tiniest bit away from them. Funny, Randall probably didn't even know she had children. He'd never displayed the slightest interest in her. But she knew all about him, where his mother lived, what his father died of, where he went on his vacations.

What she didn't know was anything about his love life. It wasn't the kind of thing you could ask in a friendly conversation with someone you didn't like. Now here was his love life in front of her. Far too good for him, she concluded after only a few minutes. So warm and friendly, and her children seemed like nice kids, though it looked like Randall was training them to whine. Maybe this was just a casual relationship, but now Carol was talking about a trip to New York they were planning in the fall. That didn't sound so casual.

"It's a business trip for Randall. He's going to be meeting with Wilson Trust."

"Why, Randall, you haven't mentioned this at the Commission."

"No, I didn't see any reason to. Martin Wilson invited me to come up and talk with them. They're trying to figure out what to do with the land, and they thought I might have some ideas. It's nothing official. They're paying for the trip."

"Well, I'm not going to worry about it. They'd have to be crazy to try to do anything with that land now. Maybe you'll want to take that young geology professor up there with you, the one you had testify. Dr. Waites, wasn't it?"

She was just kidding, but apparently she'd hit a sore spot. Even Carol looked uncomfortable. Randall must have told her about that Commission meeting. He had no sense of humor.

Chapter Twenty-Nine

Jade reached her arm out, patted along the floor to the edge of Jasmine's sleeping bag, then opened her eyes. The birds had started singing, but the light was still dim. Must be a foggy morning. They had finished carting everything to Goodwill yesterday, keeping nothing but their two sleeping bags and the electric coffee pot, as well as what they had in the van. The room was like an empty box. The air seemed dusty with all the furniture gone. Bare walls, dirty windows she'd never noticed when the house was full.

The house was suspended between its past and its future, waiting to come to life again. She felt like an intruder. It was very quiet, not even the hum of the refrigerator. When they returned from the last trip to Goodwill, they found the electricity had already been turned off; Jade had mixed up the date when she called the power company, so the coffee pot would do them no good.

She gave a tug on the sleeping bag. Jasmine rolled over and came to rest curled against her side. They lay for a quiet while longer, Jasmine still breathing sleep, Jade staring up at the ceiling that seemed so far away in the empty room

—•—

While Jade had sublet the office and listed the house, Jasmine had been in charge of selling the truck and buying the van. And she had done them proud. The van had been traded in at Coggins Motors by a drug dealer who was awaiting sentencing. It was a glitter blue monster with two full beds and six speakers. Jasmine thought it needed a little personality, so she had painted a huge rainbow on the back. Jade laughed when she saw it; it reminded her of the old Volkswagen buses.

"We'll get old hippies crawling out of the woodwork wherever we go."

"Good. That's what we're doing. Crawling out of the woodwork."

They had packed the van the night before. There was nothing to do but shower and dress. The cold water felt good. It almost took the place of coffee, but not quite, so they decided to go to Vernell's for a last breakfast.

Biscuits with sausage gravy for Jasmine, eggs and grits with a biscuit for Jade. Pleasantly stuffed, Jade took out her wallet, but suddenly Vernell was standing by the table.

"You can put that away. You come to say goodbye. This is my goodbye gift."

"How did you know?"

"First time I saw you I knew you for wanderers. You thought you'd make a home here, but the only home you'll ever have is each other. Just you remember: you can't bloom if you don't put down roots."

They were on the road by six-thirty. Since they weren't going anyplace in particular, just heading west, there wasn't any point in traveling on the interstate. They stayed on the back roads, heading through the panhandle toward Alabama. The fog was lifting, leaving mist like a ghostly quilt on the fields.

They passed by horse farms with rolling green paddocks and low white fences. They passed mobile homes trimmed with rust. Where cows sheltered under the single wide-spreading oak in the middle of a hot pasture, they saw brown rolls of hay, as smooth and trim as if they'd been sheared. A red truck poked its nose out from an old-fashioned fence of weathered sticks, woven zigzag into each other. The dumpster by the side of the road looked as if it had been dumped itself, trash scattered in the sand around it. They passed the Hopeful Baptist Church, the Naked Lady Tavern, The Female Protective Society, and Reese's Total Social Club (For Teens Only). They passed through the still-sleeping streets of small towns, where silver-domed courthouses caught the fading colors of the sunrise. And they passed mile after mile of undeveloped land, covered with scrub oak and pine.

Jade thought of how it would be, buying one of those old houses with the wrap- around porch, getting to know the boys down at the courthouse, walking through the endless acres of scrub, dreaming a whole new town.

"Think what we could build out here."

"We're through with that, Jade. We're not building anybody's dreams anymore."

Jade watched the world passing beside them, and she watched the road in front of them, smooth and gray and even, binding the earth like a ribbon, taming it. But the earth couldn't be tamed. The sinkhole had eaten the interstate. She climbed out of her seat and into the back of the van, pulled away the carpet on the wall, and opened the small sliding panel. She took out the bag of grass and papers and rolled a joint, bracing herself against the jouncing of the van.

They were quiet for a while after they finished the joint.

Then Jasmine said, "I keep thinking about that sinkhole. Maybe it was a sign. Maybe we just weren't meant to build in the Marsh."

"Lo, a hole." Jade laughed.

"Deep down and under," Jasmine intoned.

"Up to the sky!"

"Shining…"

"And thunder…"

"The well runs dry," they hollered together. And they laughed and spoke truth and nonsense all the way to Alabama.

—•—

Tyler came down the stairs and stepped into a soft gray world. The fog hid the treetops. It rolled along the street, rising and falling. Even the sun was defeated, barely shining, dim and flat as a daytime moon. Foolish, even dangerous, to ride his bike on a morning like this, but he loved to ride in the mysterious light, all color lost. It was still early, not much traffic. His bike had a headlight, and he could stay on the sidewalk most of the way.

It was a dream world, where objects rose suddenly in front of him and disappeared behind. He arrived at the plaza with no sense of distance traveled or time passed. The thick trunks of the oaks were black and wet below, but as they rose in the air they became shadowy forms and disappeared. On the benches the street dwellers were still holding on to sleep as best they could, covered by fog-dampened newspapers.

Tyler paused in front of the Commission building, looking for the words, as he always did when he passed the plaza. They glowed through the thick fog. He read them several times, puzzled.

> Deep down and under
> Up to the sky
> Shining and thunder
> The well's run dry.

They had changed. He still didn't understand them, but he had a feeling that a sentence had been carried out.

—•—

It was early still. He rode to the Punchbowl and found his favorite spot on the edge. He settled down on his poncho, and sat very still, watching a robin and a woodpecker uneasily sharing a dead tree. The woodpecker flew off and landed in a tree a few yards away, then returned, taking a branch a little higher than the robin's. The robin puffed up and began to sing. A squirrel on the next tree arched his tail and chattered furiously.

He thought of Carol and Christopher and Robin. Carol greeted him every morning at the front desk the way she always had, with a bright smile and friendly hello. It was as if she had retreated behind a glass door and shut it between them. Robin and Christopher were nothing more now than pictures on her desk, their hair neatly combed, Robin standing behind Christopher with a maternal hand on his shoulder. These three people he had known, and loved, were as hidden now as the caverns in the limestone below.

He gazed out across the sinkhole, but his view was cut short by the full crowns of the trees. It was hard to believe that this had ever been a desolate bowl of rubble like the Marsh. But even at the Marsh, the plants were beginning to take over. On his last visit he had seen them in every crack and fissure. Poking up from under the piles of broken earth, through the twisted tangles of uprooted trees, green shoots were finding the light. In a few hundred years, it would be a sunken forest.

The Ancients

The harvest moon hung low, huge and orange. Vernell looked across the plaza at the words, shimmering and sparkling in the light. She walked toward them. As she passed the fountain, the water began to flow and rose up in its dance. She came nearer still, and the words began to change. Avestan and Carian, Etruscan and Lepontic, Meroïtic and Phrygian ... Vernell faced the glowing stone, and sang the words in every lost language that appeared, her voice deep and clear.

Night creatures paused to listen. The possum stopped a moment in her climb, and her babies peeked out from their pouch. The owl veered away from the mouse and swept back up to the big live oak. The mouse lay still, heart pounding. And every living thing heard the shuffling, plodding, tramping of ancient feet, as the ancestors crossed the plaza and gathered behind Vernell.

Leptomeryx, small and elegant as a gazelle. A giant tortoise, the huge mound of its shell patterned like a quilt, stretched its neck toward the song. A thirty-foot crocodile lay curved around them, eyes glistening. Behind them stood Mesoreodon, bulky body on skinny legs, mouth in a permanent scowl, its booming howls silenced on this night. Barbourofelis, the sabre-tooth cat, with its powerful muscles and deadly teeth, stood peacefully next to three-toed, round-eyed Miohippus, while Teleoceras, a two-ton rhino with stumpy legs, lumbered up beside them. Aepycamelus tiptoed toward the rear on stilt-legs, its long neck stretching over the

226

smaller beasts, followed by the three-hundred-pound flightless Titanis Walleri, huge curved beak stained with blood. Next to it the giant armored Glyptodont twitched its pointed snout. And behind them the sloth, standing on its hind legs, towered fifteen feet above them all.

Already extinct, the beasts had nothing to fear, and prey stood next to predator, listening in silence to the mournful earth-song. Vernell sang through the night until the moon and stars began to fade and the horizon glowed golden. Then her voice fell silent, her body sank to the ground, and her spirit rose and drifted away toward the Marsh, followed by the ancestors. The rising sun shone on them and then through them until they were nothing but mists of memory.

Acknowledgments

I am grateful to all my family and friends who have cheered me on in the long, aspiring years. But I must especially thank:

Sandra Gail Lambert, a generous writer-friend to so many, who taught me by example the discipline and methodical persistence required to share our work with the world.

Joan Leggett, the editor I have always dreamed of. She helped me make my work the best it can be, and every major change she suggested was exactly right.

My husband Joe Jackson, who shared my excitement when Twisted Road decided to publish the book, took over our most complicated joint responsibility so I could focus on my work, and has supported me in every way in this new venture of being an author.

My granddaughter Ari, who cleans the kitchen and makes me laugh.

And special thanks to Lynne Rigney Barolet, a wise woman.

About the Author

Elizabeth McCulloch was born in Buenos Aires, Argentina, and lived in New England, the Midwest, Canada, and the South, before putting down roots and finding her home in Gainesville, Florida, almost forty years ago. Previously a lawyer, then a teacher, she has had children of various stripes: one born, two foster, one step, and the granddaughter she is now raising with her husband. She has been writing fiction for thirty years, and her blog, The Feminist Grandma, for eight. This is her first published novel. Webpage: elizabethmccullochauthor.com